SHATTERBUG

This is a work of fiction. Any slights of people, places, or organizations are unintentional.

First printing 2018

ISBN 978-1-7323457-0-6

SHATTERBUG

Robert Duke

01110011 01100001 01110100 01110010 01110101
01110111 01101100 01110010 01110100 01110010
01101001
01110100 01100101 01101001 01110011 01101101 01110010
01100001 01101111 01100100 01110010

Contents

Issue 1
To Die a Hero

"Power is just a fancy word for the rate of work, because as we all know, physicists have a superiority complex, otherwise we wouldn't want to be physicists." the professor said to his giggling class, deviating from his slide as he always did. "The formula for power is a lot simpler than something like power sounds like it should be. It's just work—which we just went over—divided by time. The unit for power is Watts, and apparently, we like to say that one horsepower is seven-hundred and forty-six Watts. Don't ask me, I'm just a physicist."

His class laughed again. Professor Wagner had learned a long time ago that even though most college students did honestly want to learn, it was a lot easier to do so when one felt compelled to listen closely, rather than when being told to.

"There's only a few minutes left, so I'm gonna click through the summary slides real quick so you can make sure you didn't miss writing down any of the formulas. If you think you've got 'em all, you're dismissed and I'll see you when you get lost on your worksheet that'll be in your inbox this afternoon. It pains me to go over this subject because you should have all learned it in high school, which is why I expect perfect scores from the two of you who can remember that far back." Once more, the students snickered amongst themselves and collected their things, checking the slideshow to ensure they had everything they needed. As one

1

student, Marco Nieve, began to leave, the professor asked to see him briefly.

"Marco, I wanted to see if you noticed your score from the last lab." he asked delicately.

"I did sir, and I'm sorry." the student replied with a hint of shame.

"Don't apologize, I'm asking because your test score was remarkable, and you clearly know the material; you had all the right formulas and math on your lab, it was your data that was off. Is everything ok?"

"Yeah, I'm sorry, I just— I'm not great at the execution stuff. I'm more into the theory. This lab had more steps and, I guess I just didn't follow along close enough and expected the math to save me, if that makes sense." He avoided Professor Wagner's gaze, hoping it might somehow protect him from judgment.

"I see where you're coming from, but physics isn't just about the theory. Even literal theoretical physics requires some practical application to get useful results. You're going to have to learn how to use your power—do the work. Because your test grades won't carry you if your lab grades stay like this."

"I understand. Thank you, I appreciate it." With that, Marco began to leave, but turned back to his professor again and added, "Oh, and I appreciate the pun, too!"

"Anytime, Marco." he replied, grinning.

Having no other classes today, Marco exited the engineering building and began walking down the street. It was about a ten minute walk back to the campus housing, but the afternoon sun in New Jackson wasn't so bad in winter, and the temperature never dropped below sixty. He could always appreciate the architecture on New Jackson State University's downtown campus, particularly the auditorium that he passed on his Tuesday walks back to the dorm from the engineering building.

As he walked, he began plotting his plan of attack for the final boss battle in Terminus 2 that had already forced him to reload his last game save three times. He knew if he just went back and did some side dungeons, maybe even finish the Ivory Tower questline, he could level up enough to take Ophion no problem, but that was a lot of time and effort to do something he wasn't *technically* underleveled for.

Marco was fortunate enough to have been accepted for the solitary housing units nearest the engineering building this year. Upperclassmen had first priority in applying for them, and he had been told that this opportunity was always taken advantage of, totally filling up the building. But this year, four underclassmen were able to move in without a roommate. Whether it was due to a paperwork error or just a decline in students, the lucky few weren't inclined to question it, at the risk of losing this stroke of good fortune.

Eagerly unlocking the door to his studio-apartment-like dorm, Marco carefully slid off his laptop bag, and jumped onto the couch. Turning on his controller, he loaded up Terminus 2.

Some people liked to create wild, wacky looking characters in video games, something that they don't or would never look like. Marco, however, preferred to make an avatar that looked more or less like him. He had picked a fictional race with skin tone options to match his own dark skin, afforded him by his Hispanic background. His eyes were a smidge squinted, and his mouth was firm and stoic when he wasn't emoting. The hair in the game wasn't quite right; he had short hair that spiked forward, but the closest option in Terminus 2 was mid-to-long length and spiked all

3

over like, well, like a video game character. He had a stubble not unusual for young men of Mexican heritage, but he kept it pretty low; Marco didn't think he looked very good with an actual beard or mustache.

It was a long, drawn out fight, but he'd learned from his past mistakes and kept pace with Ophion. He had the enormous dragon-god down to only a few slivers of life, and he was taking cover behind a rock formation during one of its area-of-effect attacks. Before he could prepare for a counteroffensive, however, a flash of brilliant light invaded his vision; not in the game, but *here*, in his room, just above the coffee table his feet rested upon.

When Marco uncovered his eyes, they were not focused on the television screen. Rather, they looked up at the figure now standing on the table, at Marco's feet.

The figure was seemingly a man, but no skin or bodily features were visible. He was completely covered in his peculiar outfit: it seemed to be an astronaut suit, but lacked much of the bulk. It was like a blue, or teal, or indigo; Marco didn't know or care the name of the shade. It had an unusual pattern, like pixels, fading outward toward the appendages. There were small lines, like those of a circuit board, connecting plates of some kind in various positions. On his chest, a glass window peered at a glowing cylinder. And on the man's head, a mirror-like dome, like some strange space helmet from a movie, perfectly reflecting Marco's horrified and confused face back at him.

The space man looked down at Marco, then, losing his balance, he fell forward. Marco was able to move aside with a speed that surprised even him, and the figure landed uncomfortably with his knees on the ground and his face on the couch. From this angle, Marco could see some serious damage had been done to the back of the suit; it was charred and scratched.

4

Deep. The man's skin was cut badly and bleeding, though held back some, having been partially cauterized by the damaged electronics embedded in the fabric.

Marco grabbed his phone from the couch's arm. He started to unhook the stranger's helmet from the suit, all the while dialing 9-1-1. He got the helmet off, but before he could press the last button to make the call, he froze. Looking back at him, bleeding slightly from his mouth, half-awake, was Marco's own face.

The space man's eyes opened wildly, and he pulled Marco close, audibly using all of his strength to do so. Marco dropped the phone in surprise, and the mysterious man with *his face* yelled in the loudest pained whisper that he could muster. "You... have to stop this! Please!"

"What do you— who are you? What are you talking about?!" Marco asked angrily.

"I wasn't able to stop it... that psychopath. That *darkness.* You need to try again. Take the suit again, be the hero. Be *Shatterbug.*"

Marco was floored and confused. Half of this man's—this doppelganger's—words weren't even registering, and the other half made no sense. "I don't understand. What do you need from me? Why me? Why... us?"

"Because... someone just like me said the same thing, when I was just like you." With that, the space suited Marco let go, his strength lost. He seemed to still be awake, but Marco was unable to get any response. He was losing him. Before he could even think about how to react, the stranger let out his last breath, and his arms fell limp. He was gone. Marco began to dial the police again, but stopped himself.

He paused for a few moments, carefully considering the situation. At best, a dead man was in his college dorm room, and there was no explanation for how he got there. At worst—Marco couldn't even begin to imagine. Honesty wasn't going to earn him any points; he knew from crime dramas that guilty people call in their crimes all the time to avert suspicion. There was no lawful solution to this.

"Okay," he began, talking to himself to stay calm, to stay sane. "What do I do here? What's the play? I can't call the police, so... I can call Miguel! No, no, that's a terrible idea. Even if he can keep a secret, this is crazy. I'm probably already in danger, I don't want him to be, too. I can't call anyone, that's out the window.

"So then, how does one hide a body? In the middle of a city... one doesn't. I guess, remove all evidence from him and dump him somewhere. But I'm not a murderer! This was an accident! And if he is me—somehow—then when he is found, there's gonna be a lot of questions for me anyway. So that solves nothing.

"I have no idea. No idea. I'm so lost. What do I do, what can I do?" he exclaimed, frustrated and desperate. He sat on the couch with his head in his hands, beside the other Marco. He looked at his other face with a sense of... not quite dread, but more than sorrow. He thought about what the man had said. He had to take the suit *again*. Be the hero. He said the same thing happened to him, was that what he meant? Was this Marco's future?

As weird as he felt leaving a dead man just lying in his room, Marco needed to contemplate and register what was actually happening. In the interest of trying to remain calm, and to sort all this out, he opened up his laptop—though he did so at his bed, turned away from the other Marco—and tried to search for any information, no matter how wild, on anything his doppelganger had said.

He started with just 'Shatterbug' as the search term. Ignoring the search engine's attempts to correct it to shutterbug, there were no helpful results. Everything had to do with music or a band of some kind.

He tried adding 'hero' to his search terms. Again, he had to assure the site he really didn't mean shutterbug. There wasn't even one result that looked remotely helpful. The top result had both search terms, but it was just about some video game, and of course, there was a typo; they actually did mean shutterbug.

For what seemed like an eternity, Marco tried to refine his search, even going so far as just describing the suit. For once, the Internet contained absolutely no information—not even false information. Shatterbug didn't exist. There was no hero, no darkness, and no one important named Marco Nieve.

He looked at the clock. He'd spent an hour trying to make sense of the situation. Meanwhile the other Marco was still dead, and whatever he was warning him about was still out there, presumably. He had nowhere to turn and no method by which to make a plan.

He was ready to give up, but a grim reminder emerged in his head, courtesy of the dead man in his living room. There was one last thing he hadn't tried yet. One more route Marco could take to find the truth. Listening to the last words of a dead man, respecting his last request, couldn't be the worst idea anyone's ever had, right?

He began to take the suit off of the man. There were hooks in strategic places to unlatch portions of the fabric, which was more like a flexible armor than like cloth. Thankfully, the body-double was wearing some light clothing underneath. Marco carefully donned the suit, getting used to the plates tapping gently at his joints and muscles. Finally, he slid the helmet over his head—making an effort to keep his hair out of his eyes in the process—and latched it to the collar of the outfit.

It was darker inside the helmet than he expected. The bubble-like visor was clear, but tinted quite a bit. He shrugged it off and began feeling around the various plates for some kind of button or switch; some way to make the suit work. As he looked around, his vision only slightly impaired on the very left and right edges, as well as just beneath his collar, he saw something. Not on the suit, but in it. Inside the helmet, in front of his mouth, was unmistakably a microphone. The suit was voice activated. Marco thought about what the man said; any words or phrases that may help. All he could remember was the name.

"Shatterbug."

The suit began to whir to life, he could feel a heat in front of his chest, and the plates across his body vibrated lightly, before everything suddenly stopped. Had he said it wrong?

"Shatterbug!" he repeated, with more force and confidence. Once again the suit began to react, only to give up, as if only half-inclined to obey. So 'Shatterbug' wasn't the word he needed, but maybe it was close.

"Shatterbolt!" he shouted proudly. Again, the suit began to respond before winding down.

"Shatterfy! Shattersuit! Shatter-on!" he yelled, growing more annoyed with each attempt. Over and over, the suit tried to turn on, and over and over it failed, quieting and calming, leaving Marco frustrated and useless.

"Shattershock?"

There it was. The suit whirred to life, the warmth in front of his chest became a passionate fire, the plates on his shoulders, elbows, knees, all vibrated furiously. The visor flashed inside the helmet, causing Marco to close his eyes in surprise— then everything stopped. The suit went silent.

When he opened his eyes, Marco saw the same thing. He looked at his living room, his bed against the far wall, the kitchen to the left. Only now, he saw it three times. Two screens, like a heads-up-display, shown on either side of the interior of the visor. Smaller, so as not to obstruct his vision, but clear. Marco was confused; what did this mean? Was it working right? Did he need to give other commands? Before he could begin to think of an answer, one of the screens moved.

Then the other.

He fell back, landing with his butt on the coffee table behind him, staring at the same scene he had been, while the other two screens shook wildly around, looking all over, moving about the room.

"What's going on?!" Marco shouted at no one.

"Who was that? Where are you?" replied a voice. His voice. But not from his mouth. It came from inside the helmet, a speaker beside his left ear.

"Show yourselves!" a third voice—again, distinctly his own—sounded through a speaker on his right, within the helmet.

"I don't think we can." Marco responded. "I'm Marco Nieve."

"So am I." replied the other two voices in unison.

"So, this suit makes clones?" he asked.

"Why can't we see each other, then?" asked the voice on the right.

"I— I don't know." he conceded. He looked around the room, mostly for a lack of anything else to do, settling on the wall clock which hung above his television. The other two screens did the same. As one of their gazes passed over the clock, Marco saw it.

"Wait, stop!" he exclaimed. "Look at the clock again!" The screen on the right did as it was told, and the other followed suit.

"Oh my god." the left voice said.

"*¿Que demonios...?*" the right voice concurred.

The clock Marco now stared at read 2:56 PM. But, in the left screen, he could see that the clock read 2:51 PM, and in the right, 3:01 PM.

"We can't see each other, because we're not here at the same time. It copied us five minutes into the past and future."

"Hey! The guy is gone!" the right voice observed. Marco and the left screen turned to confirm that, indeed, the other Marco was nowhere to be seen.

"Maybe we can't see him for the same reason we can't see each other. We took the suit from him, but he was still one of us. We're out of sync." the left voice thought aloud.

"We need to figure out how to get back. He has more answers!" Marco said. The others nodded their screens in agreement.

"Umm, recombine!"

The suit began to whir to life, warming and shaking, but stopped short once again. "Dammit! Why aren't there instructions for this?!"

"Keep trying!" chimed the voice to his right.

Marco did as he told himself. "Reconnect! Restart! Reinitialize!"

Time and time again the suit seemed to begin to work before it fell silent. Marco was done with trial and error. He needed answers. He needed to understand.

"Reconstitute!"

The cylinder in his chest burned with power, the plates on his shins, his forearms, his chest, began to vibrate with fervor, and with a flash from within his visor, the screens were gone. The voices were gone. Marco was alone once more in his dorm room. The doppelganger was still gone.

That evening, Marco put some dark clothes on over the Shatterbug suit, stowed the helmet in a drawstring bag, and began to walk down to the open field past the NJSU business building.

As he did, he thought about the last few hours. He didn't want to put on the suit again until he thought it was safe, and he certainly didn't want to break it, so he simply theorized about what it could be, how it worked.

Based on his experience, the cylindrical object in the chestpiece seemed to be a power supply, going from the way it heated up when activated. The vibration of the plates was clearly important for either the duplication or the time dispersal, but how they accomplished this was beyond him. There had always been

11

theories about how time travel could be achieved, but accelerated vibration of things around the travelling object was not one of them. Was something beneath the plates performing some action, and it was simply concealed? Again, Marco was not ready to find out, for fear of breaking it; his doppelganger seemed to suggest he would need it.

Though the area was well lit, it was fairly late; classes had ended hours ago, and it was a Tuesday night. If there were any parties going on, they would be small and few. He gave the area a cursory gaze to ensure there was no one around—in such a flat area, it was both easy to check, but also easy to be surprised—and donned the domed helmet. It still felt unusual, like sitting in a compact submarine. Marco was thankful for the tinting here, as the lights overhead were large, intended to illuminate soccer games on the casual open field.

"Shattershock!" he shouted somewhat quietly, in an effort to not attract the attention of any wanderers just out of sight. The suit buzzed and cracked, and then once more he was joined by a copy of himself five minutes in the past, and another five minutes in the future.

"If we're gonna be a hero, we need to know what we're doing," began the original Marco, knowing of course that being clones, the other Marcos already knew why they were here. "So now that we've got the suit's ability down, time to practice fighting."

All three Marcos took the starting positions from the fighting videos they had reviewed online during the several hours he had free in his dorm, and began slowly following the steps. Marco found that he was doing fairly well, but noticed the screen on the left was much more unstable and unsure of itself than he. Looking at the right screen, he was impressed with how quickly and smoothly it seemed to be going through the motions. Was this an effect of the time travel? Perhaps he instinctively learned from the mistakes and unease of his past version, and his future version in turn learned from him.

"Hey Marco— er, past Marco? Watch... future Marco, see how he does it, he's doing better than both of us."

"I can't see him, you're the only screen on my right." the voice by his left ear replied. Of course, Marco thought. He could see both of them because he was in the present, between them. His past self could only see him, immediately to his future, and the reverse must be true for the future Marco.

"Alright then, uh, watch me then, and I'll watch him. We'll learn from each other."

"Why does it matter?" asked the voice to his right. "When we recombine, we'll all have this knowledge and skill, won't we?"

"But we'll master it faster and be more confident in ourselves if we practice while we're separated. You being better than me and past Marco are evidence of that." Marco replied, trying not to sound short with himself.

The Marco in the future didn't reply, but silently agreed by continuing the motions and combos they had watched and memorized, becoming faster and more forceful with each iteration. Marco became more confident watching himself do better than him, and he could see from the left screen that his version in the past was improving as well. Soon, the three were completely in sync, moving with agility and power that would have taken hours for them to master alone.

They stopped to take a short congratulatory break, but were interrupted by the sounds of an argument across the street—five minutes in the future—in the alley beside the book store.

Deciding this may be a good opportunity to test their new skills and learn to combine them with the suit's power, they carefully moved closer to investigate.

From across the street, the Marco in the future could see a fight was obviously taking place. A man was slamming his fists into a younger student who clearly couldn't fight back, keeping him pinned against the wall, punching him over and over again.

In the present, Marco saw the attacker waiting silently in the darkness of the alley, but also saw that the young man was walking this way, unaware of what would happen to him in only five minutes time.

The past version of Marco saw only the skulking man in the alley, smoking a cigarette alone.

All three decided to test their skills simultaneously, staggered across time. They each crossed the street. On the left screen, Marco saw his past self immediately begin to lay into the would-be mugger, who quickly caught himself and started fighting to defend himself.

In his time, Marco instructed the approaching young man to stay back, and tried to take on the man in the alley as well. However, he seemed to be prepared, and was already getting in his own shots with Marco, though moving more slowly, as if they'd been fighting for a few minutes.

Marco's future version was able to pull the attacker off the helpless victim, who carefully got up and began to run away. The fight in the future took much the same turn as the one in the present, but the mugger was already exhausted, and did very little to defend himself, much less hurt Marco. As the fight in the past raged on, the fight in the present became easier and easier, and finally, in the future, the man was down for the count. Once his present version had also succeeded, Marco recalled his past and future selves back, and looked down at the criminal.

"Man what was that for? What are you doin'?" he pleaded, spitting a small bit of blood across the alley.

"I'm Shatterbug." Marco replied, feeling a confidence and pride like he'd never felt before. "I'm a hero, a superhero, and you're a criminal. Get out of here, before I decide you need another lesson."

Across the river, in a darker part of the city, a man in baggy cargo pants and a grey, torn muscle shirt walked down the silent, barely lit street. Julio always liked being alone. It made him feel like everyone else was hiding from him, out of fear and respect. That was what the Del Toros were all about: respect. And if you didn't respect him, you'd better be afraid. As he approached the door to the warehouse—his castle—he pulled the keys out of his pocket, careful not to knock loose the gun tucked 'safely' into his pants.

He walked inside, feeling a slight breeze. One of the boys must have left the window in his office open. It shouldn't even be open in the first place; people are less likely to try to get into a building they think is abandoned if they have to break something to do it. But a man's gotta smoke, Julio knew that.

He opened the door to his 'office,' which was more like a man cave. He admired his couches, television, minifridge filled with cheap beer, and safe; one of several keeping the Del Toro gang's ill-earned cash in their hands. But, there was something not right. The window wasn't open.

Julio flicked the light switch, but nothing happened. He looked to the light hanging from the ceiling to find it swaying gently. It didn't even do that when the window was open, let alone when it was closed. He pulled out his gun, aiming all around the room.

"Yo who's there? You better get your sorry ass outta here, *chico*, before I have to carry it out in a bag."

A brush of air, the clink of a can on the concrete ground, and swipe over his hand later, Julio found himself in the air, an arm of some kind wrapped around his torso. He tried to punch at it, finding it to be almost slimy, but not in the wet kind of way. This kind of slimy felt *wrong*. Trying to get a clearer look at it, Julio found that he couldn't. It was pitch black. Not like the shiny, cool black of his gang's cars, or even like the black of the lightless room he hovered in now. This was like a black that shouldn't exist. It was like he was looking at a picture, and whatever was supposed to be where that arm, that *tentacle* was, had been ripped out of the world, leaving only a sheer, endless, stomach-lurching darkness.

"Julio Carillo," a voice boomed behind his head. It was horrifying, menacing; hoarse like a deformed monster, with whispers echoing itself, extending into the darkness of the room— of the thing. It growled slowly, methodically. Part curious, part condescending, its pitch and tone constantly in flux.

"Such recklessness, such ignorance, to point a weapon at an unseen foe. Or rather, to attempt to." It gave out a shrieking, reverberating sigh, which Julio could only assume was some otherworldly, evil laugh. "I will champion you."

Another black tendril appeared at the top of his vision, getting closer to his face before reaching *into* his *mouth*.

"Let your heart... rest." the voice ordered, as Julio felt the blackness *crawl* and *slide* down his throat. He gagged, trying to stop the choking, but was unable to. He could feel everything and do nothing about it; not even vomit. He tried to grab the monster's arm and pull it from his esophagus, but he couldn't get a grip on the perfect, slimy darkness.

"Let your solace pump your blood." it growled hungrily, as Julio felt the tentacle *stab* itself out of his lungs, wrap itself around his heart and *squeeze* it. Just as it was about to burst, another stab told Julio it had *entered* his heart, and he could feel the tentacle *oozing* its way into his veins, *pushing* the blood out. It dripped from wherever it could as the monster *exsanguinated* him, replacing his blood with itself.

"Let void consume you, and become truly sane... for a change." Julio tried to cry out, to scream, desperate for some release from the agony the black creature was subjecting him to. He could feel the tentacles in his veins *expand*, and as they did, his muscles were *forced* to grow, *ripping* themselves, only to be mended and filled with more of the black slimy monster. He could feel every part of him growing, his bones *fracturing*, his skull *cracking*, only to be repaired by the sadistic darkness tormenting him.

Finally, after he had become a behemoth, a shadow of his former self looming over the pool of his blood on the floor, the monster released him, satisfied with the transformation. Julio could still feel the discomfort of the slime the thing had left behind coursing through him. The horror came into full view in front of him, a mass of writhing tentacles, but just as much a void as the arms which had just released him.

17

"Become Titan Black..."

Issue 2
Titanomachy

The next day was a struggle. Marco's mind couldn't stop racing. What else could the suit do? What had killed the other Marco? If he was supposed to prepare for that, to prevent it, then how? He found himself having difficulty paying attention to his schoolwork; thankfully, it was all straightforward anyway, and most teachers had their lessons online, so he could review them later.

With only two classes on Wednesdays, and both early in the morning, Marco had the whole rest of the day to try to learn more about the Shatterbug suit, and more importantly, what to do with it. Last night had been a thrill, but from the damage the previous owner had sustained, and from the gloom-and-doom speak he relayed, stopping petty crimes before they happened was not his purpose. There was something far more sinister at play, and he had every intention of figuring out what. Just as soon as he figured out *how* to figure that out.

Once he got home, Marco decided that the best place to start was the suit itself. He laid the Shatterbug outfit on the coffee table and fished out his modest toolbox. More of a box *of* tools really, it contained only the basic things to do simple tasks; a screwdriver, hammer, level—he had nothing else though. Perhaps an attempt at preparation would be rewarded.

Once he sat down to examine the armor, however, he soon came to realize that his preparations were exceptionally lacking. There didn't appear to be any screws to remove the plates, no dials or latches to release the casing over the cylinder. It was practically all one big piece of armor, but of course the grooves and differing of material were evidence to the contrary. Marco had no idea where to begin, or how. And he couldn't pry the plates off or break the glass window. He had no way of knowing if he could undo it, or if he could, that the suit would still function. He was out of his depth.

What he needed were the right tools for the job. This was a machine, a piece of electronics. The cylinder had some sort of rock or mineral inside it, some element that he could potentially measure. What he had assumed were circuits earlier were indeed some kind of wiring or bussing. The plates, as he had discovered already, vibrated when active, either as a feature or a product of something underneath them. All things that could be worked with or explored using tools present in the engineering building.

He put the suit on, again concealing it with his clothes. "Would be nice if I could fold this visor off instead of—" he began to think aloud, before the helmet seemed to hear him. The perfectly smooth glass surface inexplicably split into four pieces, retracting back into the small bit of helmet that was left. It was practically a collar now, and even that folded yet still, down to a thick choker or necklace.

"Visor... on?" he said uneasily, testing the seemingly new command. The collar unfolded back to its original shape, and from there the glass bubble re-emerged and fit itself back together.

"Very helpful." he applauded, latching it onto the outfit and retracting it back with another repetition of the voice command.

As he exited the building, Marco started to turn left to begin his walk past the auditorium and on to the College of Engineering, but he found himself looking to the right, his attention momentarily drawn by a commotion of some kind down the street. Others around him seemed to also be curious—or concerned—about the disruption, and those that were closer, further down the street, started to turn and run the other way, towards Marco. Although he wanted to believe that it was nothing important, and that he could continue on to investigate the suit without incident, he had a sinking feeling that whatever was going on was related to Shatterbug. That was, after all, right around where he had been just last night.

He began walking in the direction of the alley he had fought the mugger in. A crowd of people was currently vacating the open field, running down the street and past Marco. As they cleared, the source of the disturbance came into view.

A monstrous figure was stomping around, smashing cars and lamps and all manner of things. Fortunately, most people had already made it clear of the area, so only emotionless street features were in immediate danger. It appeared to Marco as though he, or it, was searching for something, though he was still a few hundred feet away. Marco took this time to don his helmet.

"Visor on!" he shouted, breaking into a run towards the aggressor. With a further "Shattershock!" his suit began to stir, the heat from the strange cylinder in front of his chest warmed, and the plates across his body vibrated, as his duplicates appeared once more, shattered across time.

At this point, he was in earshot of the creature, which turned at the sound of his voice, breaking through the screams and car alarms. Marco—or rather, Shatterbug—could now see that the monster was indeed a man; a huge, hulking brute, but still clearly human. He had what seemed to be black rips tattooed across his disturbingly grey skin. His jaw was enormous, and contributed to his menacing face, but not more than the blacks of his eyes; completely opaque pools with not even the shine of the sun reflected on them. He was shirtless, and his muscles seemed to ripple, or more accurately, *crawl*, as if something else was beneath his flesh.

"You!" he roared as Shatterbug approached him, cautious but prepared. "You think you can mess with the Del Toros without getting punished, *bicho*?"

He lifted his enormous fist into the air—easily half Marco's height and twice his width—swinging it down over his target's head.

The Shatterbug in the present rolled out of the way, as his past and future selves leapt onto the unusual bodybuilder in an attempt to reach his head. In both times, however, he easily threw them aside, smashing them into the asphalt. Marco saw all of this on his visor in the present, and the three regrouped to come up with a new plan of attack.

"Maybe we can trick him? Lead him into something that'll hurt him?" suggested the Shatterbug five minutes behind.

"There's nothing here that meets that. Look at the ground, he's putting dents in concrete with *us*!" shouted the present Marco, before their foe charged into him, lifting him up and tossing him into the brick wall of the bookstore. He slid to the ground, dazed.

"What are you?" the past Shatterbug asked, yelling across the street to his version of their opponent.

"This answer your question?" he replied, slamming his fist into Shatterbug with an uppercut, sending him several feet in the air. "Name's Titan Black, *cabrón*."

The past Marco landed in the soccer field, sore and hurt, but undamaged and alive.

Future Shatterbug now took a crack at Black, attempting his past self's idea of luring him into something harder than his thick skull. He positioned himself in front of one of the cars parked on the side of the road, whistling for the oversized gangster. Titan Black turned in a rage to face him, charging at him with abandon.

"Now!" shouted the future Shatterbug, as his present self reconstituted. If the Titan Black in the future hit the car, Marco couldn't tell. He failed to realize that by returning his copies into the present, the past and future were no longer in his control.

"Shattershock!" he shouted again, leaping out of the way of another of the human tank's attacks. Once more, three Shatterbugs stood in three separate moments of time. Time had changed, however, and the car they had tried to ram their opponent into was still as it was, even in the future. "What are we gonna do? This guy's unstoppable, we're getting hammered!"

"We have to try; this thing is abnormal. It can't be a coincidence he's showed up right after we got this suit. He's our responsibility." reasoned the future Marco. In the present and future, both Shatterbugs noted that police had begun to settle on either side of the fight, a few hundred feet down the road. No doubt they were giving the indescribable monster a wide berth.

All three Marcos charged for Titan Black, and he returned the favor, crashing into them with unrivaled force. They each flew backward before landing against another parked car, denting it inwards. They were hurt and sore, practically on the edge of consciousness. The suit's armor protected them from cuts and wounds, but not from pain or impact.

Black charged for them once more while they were down. In a final act of desperation, Marco groaned.

"Reconstitute..."

At the exact moment that Black's fist connected with Shatterbug, the three versions of him were pulled back into each other from across time, and the force of that reunion sent the titan flying backwards himself, through a car into the open field. As he skidded to a halt on the browning grass, Marco was able to stand up, his energy somewhat revitalized by the reconstituting of his selves; not to mention the confidence this realization had granted him.

Titan Black grunted. "Why you little...!" He began charging for Marco again, using his forearm as a shield, intending to run him over completely.

"Shattershock!" Marco yelled out, and once more, just as the monster's arm landed on him, he balled his hand into a fist. Punching up into him with an uppercut, he called out, "Reconstitute!"

Black was thrust into the air, considerably higher than he had even sent Shatterbug earlier, only to come crashing down, landing in and cratering the asphalt.

"Shattershock!" Marco yelled again, approaching the muscled criminal before he even got a chance to stand up. He reunited his duplicates once more, landing a punch into Black's side and sending him sliding into the brick wall of the book store, which eroded somewhat but remained upright.

The monster recovered more quickly this time, though clearly still shaken. He charged towards Shatterbug again, fists balled and in the air, prepared to crush the hero. Again Marco shattered himself across time, and at the moment of impact, he extended his own fist out and downward.

"Reconstitute!" he let out with all of his strength. His copies from the past and future were pulled back into him, giving him the momentary power to punch the titan into the ground.

He lay there, dazed and defeated.

The police began to approach from either end of the street now, recognizing the battle was won.

Marco approached the villain, extending a precautionary fist. Black saw this and cried, "Hey man I give, I give! Don't kill me!" as he waved his frighteningly large hands in the air.

A large S.W.A.T. van drove up, flanked by three police cruisers, as two more came in from the other end of the road. All weapons that weren't pointed at Titan Black were pointed at Shatterbug.

"I'm sorry, man! I didn't want to do this; I didn't want it to be like this." The swollen gangster whimpered, allowing the officers to lead him into the van, which only barely contained him. No one approached Marco yet, but remained trained on him.

"Then why do it? What happened to you?" Marco pleaded with him.

"This crazy black alien thing, man. It attacked me, made me into this *monstruo*. It said it'd change me back if I called you out and brought you down." He was practically sobbing now, though no tears let out.

"We'll get you somewhere safe to undo this. Just come with us. You have the right to—" began one of the officers detaining him, before Black cut them off.

"You don't get it man, there's nothin' left to undo! That thing killed me; it stuffed me full of its *mierda* and forced me to keep going. I got nothing left to go back to."

The S.W.A.T. officers closed the doors to the back of the van. It was just Marco and the rest of the police now.

"I don't want to fight, officers. My name is Shatterbug. If I hadn't intervened, that thing would have hurt someone, probably you." he said to the assembled police, calmly. He needed to talk them down; he had no intention of letting this suit fall into anyone's hands, even the authorities, and he had no idea if it was bulletproof.

"From what that thing said, it sounds like it wouldn't have started if you weren't here." one of them replied.

"You don't understand what's going on." Marco said. Granted, neither did he. "I'm here to help, but you need to let me, and that starts by letting me go."

"Not gonna happen. Hands up, you're under arrest." The officers began to get closer, weapons trained on Shatterbug.

"*Shattershock.*" he whispered to the suit. Hearing him, it burned and vibrated, creating his two copies in the past and future. The past version returned to fighting Titan Black, but the future version looked at an empty, if damaged street. "Yes, it is."

He leapt for one of the openings between two of the officers, and each other one fired on him. Marco anticipated this, and was already part-way through shouting, "Reconstitute!"

The bullets hit Shatterbug as he reunited himself, but rather than ricocheting as Marco was afraid would happen, they instead dissolved, vaporized by the force of time being cinched back together.

He made it through the opening unscathed—and without harming any of the policemen—and ran. He separated again, and once his present self had turned just out of sight, the future Marco looked for where the police would turn to in search of him. The present Marco then dove down a different alley, escaping unnoticed. He reconstituted and lowered his visor.

He only then realized that his clothes were no longer over his suit; they had fallen off when he first shattershocked before the fight. He returned to the street and checked to ensure the coast was clear before grabbing his belongings from the sidewalk, and returning to his dorm.

Perhaps, Marco thought, it would be best to lay low for awhile before trying to learn the secrets of the Shatterbug suit again.

Minh Liu entered city hall more stressed than he had ever been in the whole of his career. He juggled four phones between himself and his assistant beside him, both walking briskly inside, trying to make sense of this 'monster battle' on the university campus in his city, and trying to calm everyone down when he couldn't even do so himself. Mayors weren't supposed to handle things like *this*, and yet here he was.

He and his assistant came barging into the mayor's office, finally having been able to get off the phones for a brief moment of respite.

"Cancel all my meetings today, we need to handle this *now.*" he ordered his secretary before she had an opportunity to even greet him. Dismissing the assistant, he retired to his office—shutting the door behind him—to think and plan as to how he was going to manage this development. A monster, a vigilante, what next?

"Hello, Mayor Liu." a voice spoke by the window, which Minh now realized was dark, like the drapes had been closed—and were somehow three layers thicker. The lights were off as well, the room was dimmed. He could still make out a silhouette at the very edge, though he couldn't make out what it was, like it kept shifting, or writhing. The voice itself was deep, booming, echoed by whispers of itself.

"How did you get in here? Who are you?" the mayor asked of his intruder.

"Oh, come now, mister mayor. You are a politician; who I am is of no consequence." it replied. Its voice was cold, slow and methodical, its volume and vibrato changed with each overextended syllable. "The only question you care about is this: what do I want?"

The silhouette quickly skirted across the room, its full shape looming over the terrified mayor, who could now see and understand that it was not a silhouette. The being was without color or form, its outline indiscernible as its many tendrils wriggled effortlessly, as though carried by a light breeze.

"The answer to that question then, is the same thing as you, for this city: solace, at last. And by my instruction, you will provide that to the people you serve. If you do not, Minh Liu, your legacy will end, your city will hate and discard you, and you will breathe no more."

Issue 3
On the Clock

It had been several days since Marco did anything with the suit. He should have felt relaxed and relieved, but instead, he simply felt burdened. He was stressed from the secret he had to keep, and from the fear of whatever thing Titan Black was working for. It told him to take Shatterbug down specifically. Was it after the suit? How did it know where it was? None of these questions were any closer to getting an answer, and he still had no explanation as to how the suit worked or where it came from.

Marco snapped. He'd had enough of lying low, of waiting. The following Tuesday, after his physics class, he returned to his dorm. He enjoyed the walk past the auditorium much less than usual today; he was on a mission. Alone in the studio, Marco packed the Shatterbug outfit into a drawstring bag, put on the folded-back visor, and returned to the College of Engineering.

Marco was by no means a criminal, but even he knew that the key to sneaking into a place is not to avoid being seen. Rather, it was to be seen and not noticed. The most effective way to do that was also the simplest: act like you belong. Walk with a sense of purpose. Don't shift your eyes, don't turn corners too quickly or even act overly polite to the people walking around you. Walk like you are going somewhere, to do something, and like it is important, like it is expected. Then, no one will pay any attention. So he did just that, looking for an empty lab, checking schedules to

29

see if a class would be using it soon. Once he found a secure-looking one—Lab Room 12—he locked the door and moved to the far end of the room, where he couldn't be seen from the door's window.

The windows in the lab rooms were all small and close to the ceiling. They were less for emergency egress, as there was an outward-opening door for that, and more for airing out any buildup of harmful chemicals in conjunction with the air system. In the corner, Marco had no reason to suspect he'd be observed.

He pulled the suit out from the bag, opened the visor, and laid them both out on one of the long tables.

Using some precision forceps, he was able to carefully grab onto the metal casing around the glass window in the center of the chest plates. It rotated in place, but rather than unscrewing itself, the panel turned and slid aside. The window became an opening, revealing the strange cylinder-encased rock.

Again, with the forceps, Marco gently removed the tube, which snapped out of position like a battery, and moved it carefully over to the mass spectrometer. This one wasn't particularly flashy, barely larger than a minifridge. But Marco didn't need a detailed rundown; he just needed to know in general what he was looking at, what he was working with—to start with, at least.

"*Dios ayúdame*, please don't let this ruin everything." he prayed, turning on the mass spectrometer and letting it examine the mineral sample.

The machine whirred and bleeped, relaying that it was working. He couldn't see the sample, but surely if it was being damaged, the machine would inform him.

After a few tense minutes, it finished. Marco took the sample out and returned it to the cylindrical casing before even thinking about the results, checking for any faults. It appeared to be fine, though he would need to test the suit again to be sure. Before that, though, he turned to the screen on the machine.

The display caused him to rub his eyes. Then to rub the screen. Then to poke at it to try to get it to show something more useful. But the results never changed.

"*¿Que demonios...?*"

The sample was one-hundred percent Element 120. But that was impossible. It was only hypothetical; all attempts at synthesizing it thus far had been failures. There was no way it could be here. And yet he held it in his hand: a pure, undiscovered element.

But the question remained: how did it work? How did this element—which should simply be an alkali earth metal—allow for time travel, for cloning and reuniting people? What else was the suit hiding?

Marco found another tool with which to carefully pry off the plate on the suit's left shoulder. His hypothesis was correct: it concealed a piece of machinery. It was fairly flat, adorned with tiny LED bulbs and small parts which clearly moved when activated. He didn't understand any of it. He may have classes in the engineering building, but he was a physicist, not an electrical engineer. He understood the theory of electronics, he could read circuit diagrams, but beyond that, he was blind.

He carefully fitted the plate back onto the outfit's shoulder. It snapped into place with some teeth poking out from the machinery it protected, and seemed to be held there even further by magnets along the edge.

Up until now Marco had been adamant, if indecisive, about involving anyone else in this Shatterbug business. Now, however, he found himself at an impasse.

"I need help," he admitted to himself. "I need someone who knows what they're doing, who I can trust. Not a friend, that's too dangerous. It has to be a stranger. But how can I trust someone I don't know?"

He returned the glass panel protecting the Element 120 container to its original position, stowed the suit away once more, and made way for his dorm. He continued to think to himself on the walk back. What were some ways to ask for help? To find a person he could trust with little risk? Online forums were certainly out of the question; even if he could reach the right people safely, it would be too challenging to connect and work together. Someone local would be preferred. He couldn't very well go on television, in costume or otherwise. That would be too public, too dangerous. There had to be a low-key option, some way to reach the right people, but stay under the radar.

He looked around the street, mostly idly. That was when he saw it, and it struck him: newspapers. They were archaic, but still around. At worst, it wouldn't go anywhere, but if he could reach just that one person who read them, who could help him...

That was it. Marco would look for other ways to reach out as well, but at the very least he could run a small blurb in the classifieds. They were put up on their websites as well, so really that was two avenues covered. He needed to be discreet though, he couldn't submit it online. He'd need to pay cash, at the paper's office.

With some brief research on his smartphone, Marco decided on the New Jackson Republic for his news source of choice. Thankfully, there was a Valley Metro station just up the street from the College of Engineering, and so he turned on the spot and walked back the way he came and up to the train stop. He went over the directions to himself while he waited there for the next light rail to arrive, in about seven minutes.

"Ok, I'll ride the train to Washington and Third, then walk north two blocks, along Third Street. Then I turn left and it's practically right in front of me; easy." Marco always struggled with even simple directions, but it was hard to get lost in a city so dedicated to grids and efficient signage. Once he'd gone over it a few times, the light rail arrived, and he felt confident in his spatial awareness. Marco thought it funny how easily time travel came to him when moving around the city was still so stressful.

The Republic Media building was not the tallest in the area. It wasn't even the biggest on the block, though it was the most impressive at the intersection. Marco walked through the doors on the corner of the glass building, flanked on either side by parked news vans. There wasn't much foot traffic here, even from the hotel right nearby.

The secretary was polite and helpful. Marco was expecting a little more resistance, but he handed him a form and gestured him to some benches to fill it out. When Marco finished, the gentleman put his payment in an envelope and thanked him for coming in, all with a smile. Some inhabitants of New Jackson were less than admirable, but one could always leave it to the people answering phone calls and directing guests to appointments to restore one's faith in humanity.

The message he decided to leave was concise, for more reason than the price per word. He had to be specific in his needs without giving too much away, for fear of being found out by the wrong kind of people. This and his contact information should suffice. They would have to, anyway.

PHYSICIST SEEKING ENGINEER FOR

LUCRATIVE COOPERATIVE PROJECT

Once Marco had finished up there, he turned to leave, once again checking his phone to ensure he knew where he was going to board the light rail back.

Before he made it to the door, however, four men with black military gear, masks, and drawn rifles darted inside.

"Everyone on the ground!" ordered one of the attackers. Marco silently cursed himself for not having the suit on under his clothes, and so had no choice but to obey. He put his arms up and lay down, keeping his chin elevated so as to see what was going on. Everyone else followed suit. The secretary remained in his chair but held his arms in the air, away from the desk.

The first man directed with his hand for two of the others to remain here, as he and the fourth attacker entered the elevator and took it up to the top floor. Several minutes passed; the two criminals guarding the assembled citizens watched for any sudden movements. However, they were not jittery, not looking for a reason to open fire. They were cautious and trained.

After six minutes, the elevator doors opened, and the two men emerged with a woman. Her arms appeared to be tied behind her back, and the two men dragged her by her elbows. Her head was covered by a black sack.

"Target acquired, let's move. Everybody stay down! We're done here unless you make a stupid mistake." barked the first man again. They stepped outside and into the waiting van, which ran the red light and drove off down the street.

Once they had left, everyone began scrambling. Reporters that had been in the room started calling the people upstairs, the secretary was dialing for the police, and everyone else was phoning their families. Everyone had a device in their hands, except for Marco.

He sprinted into the bathroom, quickly taking off his clothes and slipping on the Shatterbug armor and closed visor. He put his clothes back on over it to ensure no one got immediately suspicious, and ran outside, down the street in the direction of the van.

"Visor on! Shattershock!" Marco shouted in succession, as the suit sparked itself to life. On his display appeared the two screens of his duplicates in the past and future. He began picking up his clothes in the present to stuff into his drawstring bag, and the past Marco watched for the van to pass.

Just as they had five minutes before, the abductors ran the red light at the intersection in front of Republic Media, and sped past Shatterbug. Though they were in a vehicle, traffic was still heavy enough that they couldn't drive too quickly, weaving through the lanes though they were. The Shatterbug in that time kept pace with them on the sidewalk, skipping around the few scattered pedestrians. The other two Marcos followed the same course in their own times.

In the past, the van went through two more lights and then turned left. All three versions of Shatterbug were still at the second intersection at the time.

"Past Marco, keep following their route." started the present Shatterbug. "Me and future Marco will take a shortcut. Let us know if they turn again!" As instructed, the Marco in the future turned left along with his copy in the present.

Once they were almost to the intersection, the Shatterbug furthest back in time spoke up. "They turned left again, the very next light! They should pass you any moment!"

Indeed they did. When the present and future Marcos arrived at the light, the van made a screeching right in the original time. It had to go slower here, as traffic was heavier, but the Shatterbugs still couldn't quite catch up with it. They saw it turn left again—if Marco wasn't mistaken, onto Washington Street—but then all three lost sight of it.

Still, they proceeded down to Washington Street, where in the past, they saw the men already having exited the van, inside the Skyrise Northeast building and entering its elevator.

They began to try and run inside, but before they made it across the street, the monitor in the plaza began to ring with an emergency broadcast, five minutes in the future.

The mayor was speaking to the city.

"Citizens of New Jackson." he began, his face of sweat and concern unconcealed by the camera. Marco didn't know much about the mayor; he wasn't particularly politically active. He knew his name was Minh Liu, but of course the card at the bottom of the screen was there to remind him. "As you know, ten minutes ago, several business and political officials were kidnapped in a simultaneous, coordinated attack across the city. Their abductors have just called me; they have confirmed for me that the victims are alive, and have given me instructions to facilitate their safe release.

"The kidnappers have assured me that they will release the hostages if the vigilante known as Shatterbug turns himself over to them. Should any law enforcement agents enter the Skyrise building, or should Shatterbug not give himself up in the next half hour..." he paused, not wishing to specify the consequences. "We do not negotiate with criminals. However, as myself and the Sheriff work with law enforcement to determine an appropriate course of action, I feel I would be remiss to not turn to Shatterbug in this moment. I beg of you, New Jackson begs of you, if you are indeed a hero, if you truly want to help this city, then please help these people. Give yourself over to these criminals. End this hostage crisis, and let us bring these men to justice. For the rest of you, I'd ask that all of you remain calm. If you are in the area or in the building, please stay where you are and assist our law enforcement officers by keeping yourself safe. And if those people being held against their will can hear me, sit tight. Thank you."

Marco didn't know what to say, none of them did. Unfortunately, once the people in the future recognized that Shatterbug was there, they had no time to be frozen. All three ran into the building, but the future version was chased in. Even after he got through the doors, a mob followed him inside. Only one word came to mind in all three times.

"Reconstitute!"

At first everything seemed normal. He was whole again, back in one time, and the mob of people hadn't yet formed. And yet Marco felt odd, like he was missing something.

Inside the building, it was chaos. Which made sense; several groups of armed men had just come in with guns held to captive officials. But, in the present and future, moments ago, the lobby was empty. It was only in the past, when the kidnappers had just come through, that people were still around, still scrambling.

This was in the past. Marco was in the past.

How did he miss it? In his haste, in the confusion, he hadn't given the command in the present; it was his past self which shouted reconstitute. And so all three Shatterbugs had been pulled five minutes into the past!

"It really is a time travel suit." Marco mused. This was a game changer. He now had less than ten minutes before the mayor's announcement, which meant just less than forty minutes to rescue the hostages.

He could see from the display that the elevator they had entered was currently on floor twelve. No one else would have used it in the past few moments of panic, so it was practically guaranteed that was where they were. Shatterbug thought it best not to take the elevator, or they'd be waiting for him, ready to gun him down before the doors had even opened all the way. The stairs were safer, and he had a large window of time anyway.

He shattershocked again while climbing up the stairs. To be sure he truly understood what he thought had happened, Marco attempted to reconstitute in the future.

He had reunited, certainly, but without a watch or anything to check, he couldn't be sure. He parted ways again, this time coming back together five minutes in the past from that point, back where he started. It seemed to be working well enough. He supposed he would find out.

Once he reached the twelfth floor, he whispered for the suit to shattershock again. All three of his selves peered through the door. The floor was empty, not leased out to anyone yet. He could see the hostages—bags still over their heads, lined up against the window. In the past, it seemed the mercenaries had just finished sitting their targets into position, and were pulling up some chairs that were set against the wall. In the present, one of the men was making a phone call. Presumably to the mayor, though Marco couldn't hear. He closed his phone quickly, though, and placed it in one of the pockets of his vest. In the future, it seemed the men were patiently waiting for the clock to tick down; weapons drawn, but well behaved.

Marco hoped he was right as all three versions stepped into the empty room. They stood in their respective times as if they were beside each other, rather than in the same position. The criminal leader spoke first.

"Turning yourself in, bug boy?" he taunted to Shatterbug in all three times, though the present Marco was more focused on his time than the others'.

"I'm taking the hostages with me, and you are turning yourselves over to the police." Shatterbug responded confidently.

"Like Hell you are. Kill 'im." replied the leader.

In the heat of the moment, with adrenaline rushing into Marco's brain, time slowed to a crawl. This wasn't a power of the suit, this was a power of the mind, thinking and calculating faster than it ever had before, faced with mortal danger. In that moment, in which one of the riflemen fired on Shatterbug in the present, all three Marcos registered it.

The Marco in the past shouted, "Reconstitute!"

The suit obliged, pulling his present self, and the future version, back in time and out of the way of the bullet.

Reunited, Marco called out, "Shattershock!" Once more, three copies existed in three moments of time.

Another bullet fired in what was now the present. Future Shatterbug took a step forward and commanded, "Reconstitute!"

Time was forced back together, reuniting his three selves five minutes in the future.

Shatterbug split himself apart. A bullet fired in the present. The future Marco took a step towards the shooters, then folded his selves forward through time, back together, before shattering again, hearing gunfire again, stepping forward again, and reconstituting again in a different time. Each iteration taking Shatterbug a step forward, closer to his attackers, dodging bullets by jumping in and out of the past, present and future; dodging time itself.

Eventually, Marco was close enough to reach out towards one of the gunmen. Over three iterations, Marco was able to subdue him, continuing to dodge the bullets of the other men firing on him. Once he was disarmed in all three moments of time which Shatterbug kept jumping in and out of, he moved on, again stepping towards another of the criminals, dodging their bullets by reconstituting in a different time than they were shooting, and repeating this process.

Finally, only the leader remained. Shatterbug was unharmed, as were the hostages, all ducking for cover from the gunfire. Marco reached him—if he was keeping track properly, about ten minutes after the mayor's public statement—and knocked him to the ground with a decisive "Reconstitute!" putting all of the force of time rippling back to one Shatterbug into his punch.

"Who are you punks?" Shatterbug asked of the leader, now down and disarmed but still conscious.

"We're hired guns kid," he grunted, spitting to the side. "It's just a job. Don't know who these people are, don't care to know."

"Who hired you then?" Marco demanded.

"There's this thing, maybe you've heard of it, called confidentiality. A certain amount of money pays for it in this business."

"Well, maybe I'll just see what your phone has to say about it then. I assume it's a burner?"

The man's poker face was nonexistent. He'd been had, and he knew it. Shatterbug reached into the man's vest pocket and pulled out, as he suspected, a simple flip phone. No lock screen, no special backgrounds or apps. He checked the call history and saw only one phone call had been made. Marco hit redial, and put the device on speaker.

"Hello?" answered a voice. It sounded a little different over the phone, but its identity was unmistakable.

"Did he show up yet, do you have him?" Marco didn't respond. "You shouldn't be calling me if you haven't got him yet."

Marco hung up. He had all he needed.

Mayor Liu sat impatiently in his office. There was no word from the thugs he had hired—although he was sure that they'd called a few minutes ago—and the Sheriff wasn't keeping him in the loop after the stunt he'd pulled with the public statement; but what choice did he have?

Shatterbug, or whoever he was, had only a few minutes left to surrender to the mercenaries. Minh wasn't sure what that *thing* wanted so badly with some vigilante. It was clearly strong enough to take care of itself, too, so why was it making him do all this work? It was risky—for him, anyway. He heard footsteps outside. Hopefully the police had broken through and rescued everyone. That thing could hardly fault him for local law enforcement acting of their own accord, could it?

The doors burst open. The mayor was correct, it was the police. Unfortunately, Shatterbug was with them, and not in handcuffs. Minh knew where this was going, but sat in his chair to play this out. Maybe he could walk away from this; he was, after all, their beloved elected official.

"Shatterbug, what are you doing here? I think you misunderstood, you're not surrendering to me, you need to go to the kidnappers to free the hostages! Unless... have you rescued them?"

"The hostages are safe, and their abductors have been arrested." one of the officers beside the vigilante answered. "But according to Shatterbug, there's one more criminal that needs to go down."

"So then why are you not out there arresting them, officer?"

"Cut the act, mister mayor." Shatterbug replied, angrily. "I know you hired those mercs. You put innocent people in danger to take me out—for what? I've done one thing: protect a street of students from a 'roided-up lunatic. How is that worth killing me over?"

"I assure you, I have no idea what you are referring—"

"We've seen the phone, Mayor Liu." interrupted the officer. "You are under arrest for conspiracy, seven charges of kidnapping, abetment; it'll all be at the precinct for you. You have the right to remain silent. You have the right to an—"

"Yes, yes, thank you officer." Minh cut him short. He turned to Shatterbug. "I'm not getting out of this, I know that. If it means anything, though, I did what I thought I needed to for this city, and yes, for myself. It was nothing against you, and it wasn't my idea. But if I were you, I would watch my back very closely. Something out there is very interested in seeing you fail. Officers."

With that, the Mayor of New Jackson was escorted from city hall in handcuffs, and Shatterbug was left alone in the office to contemplate the day's events, and what they might mean going forward.

From atop city hall, a small, void-like creature looked down at the scene below. Its temporary lackey, Mayor Minh Liu, was being hauled away in a police vehicle. The hero Shatterbug exited the building, watching the reluctantly obedient politician be driven off.

"You are more resourceful and quick-thinking than I expected." it began. Its words were carefully chosen, its tempo slow, enjoying each syllable of the primitive language it now spoke aloud. No one could hear it, of course; it spoke to itself for its own amusement. "It would seem I will need to be more… unorthodox in my methods. Some trial and error will evidently be required before I can triumph. But do not fret, Marco Nieve. You need not be burdened with such trifles as responsibility for too much longer."

It cackled to itself in its twisted, shapeless way: a reverberating sigh stretched through its void and shrieking with mirth, mocking the city—the world below—in all its ignorance.

Issue 4
Unclear Signs

Early Wednesday mornings were rarely busy in New Jackson. In general, the rush hour began at around six o'clock, and Geoffrey was always particular about leaving for work at five. In part to beat the morning traffic, and in part because his work demanded it; or to be more accurate, he demanded it of himself for his work.

However, this Wednesday morning was not typical. The whole city had practically turned upside down the previous day, after all. One would be surprised if there were not more traffic, angst, and confusion. Everyone was excited and on edge. News crews were scattered across the city, even in places where there had been no kidnappings, nowhere near city hall or the Skyrise building.

As such, Geoffrey's peaceful twenty-minute drive became a frustrating hour-and-fifteen-minute ordeal, as he crossed the downtown area early that Wednesday morning.

Finally, though, he arrived. He always suspected this location had been chosen with the idea that it wasn't much to look at. It was a rather large warehouse, with stark white concrete walls and an impressive—yet empty—parking lot. Perhaps the only interesting thing about it was that it was inexplicably spared of any graffiti or vandalism in the three years it had been empty.

To Geoffrey, however, it had always stood as a monument. He saw it for what it contained, what it would mean; even if it would never be known for it.

He drove his car around to the back, where a loading dock hid a garage door, held closed by an adjacent locked box. He opened the car door and approached the box, turning his personal key in the lock and swinging the panel open. After pressing the now revealed button and returning to his still running vehicle, he drove his car inside and parked it among the others. Of course, they had arrived before him—only he should be so unlucky.

"Good morning, Doctor Strauss." one of the engineers greeted as he walked into the office space that had been propped up within the expansive interior. "Traffic hit you bad?"

"Morning, Doctor Wheeler. Yes, it was awful." he replied, setting his file case beside his desk. He joined the others in the control room. "I still cannot comprehend the level of... inhumanity of some people. I'd be interested to see an experiment done on whether weaving through heavy traffic is any faster than staying in one lane the whole time. Because until I do, I can only conclude that it isn't, and therefore, that people are assholes."

Doctor Wheeler chuckled with genuine amusement. Doctor Renault and Mister Hacking agreed with Geoffrey, nonverbally approving of his conclusion. As always, Doctor Lauren James prattled on with an insufferable tale that was only tangentially related to the topic at hand—Geoffrey assumed this was some mechanism to feel included or important, but it only served to make her seem a child begging for attention. Still, she knew her neuroscience, if nothing else.

"Have we started prepping the machine?" Doctor Strauss asked his team.

"Yes, it's at seventy-two-percent charge right now." Doctor Ken Wheeler replied. He was an excellent mechanic, renowned in certain circles for his ingenuity in taking engineers' designs and improving them as a second nature during fabrication. "I just finished inspecting the rotors; the fix we put in last week is holding up very well, I don't think we'll need to worry about internal snagging anymore."

"Has our subject arrived yet? I didn't see a new car." noted Geoffrey.

"No, he still has fifteen minutes though. He seemed like he thought the pay was worth it; I don't think he'll skip out on us." answered Edwin Renault. Although Doctor Strauss was the project lead, Doctor Renault put the most work into the machine's functional designs. Geoffrey couldn't be more grateful that his old friend was willing to join him, and that their benefactors were open to the suggestion.

"I should hope so," Jeremiah Hacking chortled. "We're paying him nearly as much as we make in a day."

"It's not our money, Jeremiah." Strauss retorted shortly. "If our benefactors see fit to offer such a large stipend to get results, we should be nothing but grateful."

Mr. Hacking huffed in declaration of his unwillingness to continue the conversation, and returned to his paperwork. There was no doubt he was the best at interpreting complex data like what their machine put out, and he worked well with Doctors James and Renault to improve results. But every so often Geoffrey wondered if having the best was worth a superiority complex.

Over the next twenty minutes, Jeremiah talked with Edwin and Ken as they continued to tune the dials on the machine's control panel using yesterday's data. Lauren and Geoffrey eagerly awaited their subject's arrival, watching the exterior cameras for any new vehicles. Finally, the machine reached one-hundred percent charge, but their human trial-goer had yet to show.

"Should we give him a few more minutes?" Lauren finally asked.

"We can't afford it. Do you have any idea how dangerous it is to keep the machine running?" Mister Hacking said patronizingly.

"Relax, Jeremiah." Geoffrey tried to calm the tension before Lauren could make it worse. "The traffic was heavy this morning; he may very well be running late."

"I can call him, see how much longer he'll be." offered Doctor Renault.

"I don't think you grasp the severity of waiting. Not only is it dangerous to leave the machine on and charged, if he doesn't show then we have nothing to work with! A wasted day! Our benefactors will not stand for it!" Hacking was nearly shouting now.

Before Geoffrey could respond, Doctor Wheeler calmly stepped into the debate. "He's right. We call it one-hundred percent charged, but the machine doesn't have a physical cap. It'll keep charging until it rips itself apart."

Everyone was looking to Doctor Strauss. He wasn't sure what to say; if he didn't know any better, he'd say it was a mutiny.

After a few silent moments, he spoke up.

"Ken," he began. "How sure are we that the machine is safe to run, physically?"

"Well, uh," Doctor Wheeler was caught off guard. "It's unlikely to have any mechanical issues, if that's what you mean. At this point it's just a matter of getting the finer things tuned to get the results we need."

"And how close are we to substantial results, Edwin? Jeremiah?"

"Um, it's hard to say." answered Doctor Renault. "Every dial we turn affects every other dial in some way. It could literally be anywhere between one and seven-hundred more attempts before we see any progress. Ballpark minimum."

"Would a diagnostic help with that at all? An empty test seat?"

"I uh— I suppose it couldn't hurt. It wouldn't yield any neurological data, but looking at the levels of a blank run could help reduce our trial count to three-hundred or so."

"Is that okay with you, Doctor James? No brain scans today?"

"I suppose I can go one day without looking at pictures of brain activity, Doctor Strauss." Lauren replied. "But what about our benefactors? They want thorough data—full reports."

"They are going to have to deal with what they can get. Without a test subject, our options are to shut down the machine and give them nothing for today, or run a diagnostic experiment and give them a faster timetable. The former guarantees we lose our funding. At least the latter gives us something to make a case with. And I'm giving you all my express permission to throw me under the bus to keep this project from getting tanked, even if it means I will be."

There was an unsuredness about the room. Only Jeremiah seemed unconcerned with the plan, and as he returned to his work, the others followed suit, following their project lead's orders. Once the dials were set and the command window was online, Doctor Strauss nodded to Doctor Wheeler, and the machine began to run with an empty seat.

Various whirring and grinding noises could be heard from the machine's test room, visible from the observation window in the control room. Most of their office space was no better than a movie prop, but the room containing the enormous machine was like a vault, protecting everyone outside of it more than protecting their work from intruders. To that end, the window was not perfect, and so no one saw the strange, lightless tendril lurking in the high corner of the room, largely concealed by part of the machine.

"Such admirable compassion, to concern yourself with your subordinates' livelihoods over your own." it spoke to itself, aware that no one else could hear it over the rumbling of the primitive metal box beneath it. Its voice was cold, filled with condescension and bemusement. It could not settle on a tone, adjusting itself slightly with each elongated syllable. "I am curious, what will you accomplish, when the roles are reversed?"

The unreflective, tentacled being quickly and silently ripped and sliced at the metal cover on the back of the machine, reaching inside the small hole it punctured and grabbing at any and every loose wire, turning rotor and mashing gear. To an observer, if there were one, it would appear as chaos. But, the entity was acting entirely with method and purpose.

The people observing the diagnostic run in the next room could tell something was wrong, but were blinded to the cause. Before they could attempt to do anything to halt the experiment or resolve the meltdown, it was too late. Doctor Geoffrey Strauss saw only the shattering of the three-inch glass window at the hands of a great fireball, before his vision went black and his body went limp.

Television and movies have led people to believe that waking up in a hospital is immediately terrifying. That the instant one realizes where one is, one feels the need to rip off any important tubes or wrappings, jump out of bed, and escape.

Geoffrey, however, awoke calmly and peacefully. Looking up at the well lit ceiling and around at the IV station told him he was in a hospital room, safe and alive. He had no reason to be terrified.

What he did feel, after a few moments, was horror.

When he felt that there were bandages covering his whole body, that the coarse—yet fluffy—fabric was right up against his head, alluding to his new lack of hair, he didn't want to run, didn't want to escape. He wanted to curl up and hide, to go back to sleep, to wake up from this nightmare.

But the nurses moving about outside his room were not familiar. He didn't recognize the man in scrubs changing his IV's fluid bag. These were not fabrications from his memories; he was not dreaming.

Geoffrey let out a sigh of defeat.

"Oh, you're awake! Just relax sir, I'll go fetch Doctor Ford." the nurse said calmly and politely. That was his job, after all. He exited the room, having finished his initial chore.

Geoffrey spent the next few minutes trying to determine what had happened. He could tell he had a concussion, though discerning the severity was not within his authority. He remembered the machine misbehaving, and ordering Doctor Wheeler to shut it down. Then the explosion; before Ken had the opportunity to react, the window was blown open, right in front of him.

That fireball. There was no way Ken could have survived. Jeremiah and Lauren were off to the side, and Edwin was standing right next to Geoffrey, in the back of the control room. Surely at least they were alright, if he was. Though he wouldn't be terribly concerned if Jeremiah didn't make it.

His doctor entered the room before he could try to remember any further. She approached the side of the bed, a tablet held out a bit from her waist for her to see. She looked up after her brief overview of its information.

"Good to see you awake, Doctor Strauss. My name is Doctor Ford, you're at the City of New Jackson General Hospital. How are you feeling?"

Geoffrey was so caught up with trying to understand what had happened that he forgot to even consider his present state.

"Sore, I think, but it doesn't seem like anything's broken. Not that I can move with all these bandages."

"Excellent assessment; you're right, nothing is broken. I don't like to use the word miracle often, but you were certainly very lucky. There also don't appear to be any serious burns, and your concussion is fairly mild, though we do have you on some painkillers."

"Apologies, Doctor, I wasn't clear. I meant to ask: if nothing's broken, why the bandaging?"

"What do you remember about what happened?"

Geoffrey wasn't pleased with her avoiding the question, but decided to play along. "There was an accident; an explosion." He couldn't give too many details, given the work he was doing.

"That's what I'm told, yes. When they brought you in, we expected there would be widespread burns, nerve damage, et cetera. Thankfully we were wrong, but the reason we thought that would be the case is its own problem."

"I'm a doctor, ma'am. Please respect that I can be detached."

"You're right, I'm sorry." Doctor Ford hesitated. "The fire you experienced didn't burn your skin or nerves, however it did char and kill most of the melanocytes all across your body."

Strauss froze, slowly recognizing the implications of her diagnosis.

"We're still not certain how it happened, and there's no precedent for treatment or recovery. The bandages are to prevent any further skin damage, as you are now much more susceptible to solar radiation. Whether you have sensitivity to other light sources as well is something we haven't tested yet, but the bandages are precautionary in the event you do."

He looked out the window—which he now noticed had the blinds drawn—to get a glimpse of sunlight, a taste of it, if he could. But it was dark, well in the evening. "What time is it?"

"It's 9:37 PM, Thursday." Doctor Ford replied. He'd been out for over thirty-six hours.

"How do we proceed?" Although it was phrased as a question, Doctor Strauss' tone was more appropriate for a demand than a query.

"You are slated for release tomorrow morning, after you decide whether you'd like to have any further tests performed on your skin sensitivity to heat and light. Your concussion is quite mild; I'll prescribe you some stronger painkillers, but over the counter drugs should do fine after that—just keep away from ibuprofen. I'd also like you to see us as an outpatient to keep an eye on any further damage, and to offer further treatments as we learn more about your condition." Again, she hesitated. "There are also some men who were adamant on seeing you once you awoke."

Doctor Ford left Geoffrey's hospital room, but he was not alone for long. Two men in suits entered after a few moments.

"Evening Doctor Strauss." started the shorter one. "I'm Agent Jennings, this is my partner: Agent O'Brien. No questions right now, just relaying some information."

Agent Jennings flashed his badge. FBI.

"As you know, your project was being funded by the D-O-D, and while you were given unprecedented autonomy, this fiasco demands that we step in to investigate. You were the only survivor of this incident, and while we are proceeding under the assumption that this was an accident, we can't rule out that you may be guilty of criminal negligence, or worse—you understand." the first agent spouted coldly.

"You're not under arrest, but you will need to check in with us at the Bureau's office at this address." The agent motioned to his partner, who placed a card on the table next to Geoffrey's bed. "You can call the number there to make an appointment. And of course we ask you to not leave town until the investigation is complete. Oh, and while the investigation is ongoing, you are blacklisted from any other government funding, and your current project is being defunded; any materials or research that survived the explosion has been destroyed."

The two agents left Geoffrey alone once more. He had always worried about what would happen were his project shut down, but he never imagined it would go like this—or that his whole life, everything he had worked for these past few months, could be taken from him in a single conversation.

All of his research: gone.

His coworkers, friends: gone.

No government funding meant no income; he had no way to keep his apartment. His car would likely have been destroyed in the blast, and although he had insurance, he could hardly get a new one without borrowing obscene sums of credit.

Doctor Geoffrey Strauss found it hard to feel anything but defeated, as he kept himself from crying and returned to sleep.

The next morning, Geoffrey allowed for the doctors to perform some noninvasive tests to determine the extent of his new skin condition. Thankfully, incandescent and fluorescent light was not found to damage his skin any further, however the former did elicit some discomfort, and the latter: rash-like pain.

Light produced by LEDs seemed to be safe, however, and by covering up the unpigmented portions of his skin—which stretched all over his body in seemingly random, swirling patterns of dead grey skin, with only his face spared—he could tolerate even sunlight. Of course the constant insulation did present the possibility of further issues, including folliculitis and rapid epidermal decay, but there was little that could be done about that for the moment.

With prescription papers and informational documents in hand, Doctor Geoffrey Strauss was discharged from the City of New Jackson General Hospital, looking more like a mummy than a person.

It was a short distance to the bus stop, but Geoffrey was shambling along the sidewalk without purpose, without life. He was broken. He didn't look at anything—his eyes were open, but devoid of wonder or meaning. As such, he wasn't really keeping track of how long it took him to reach the bus station, how long he waited for it, how long he was on it, or how long it took him to walk from his stop back to his apartment; he just didn't care.

Doctor Strauss unlocked his front door and wandered inside. He picked up the two newspapers which had been shoved through his mail slot—not for any real reason, but it was a habit—and set them on the kitchen counter. Maybe he'd look at them later, maybe not. He wasn't picky.

Flipping on the television just bored him. Most of it registered as noise. He thought he heard something about the mayor's case but wasn't interested enough to retain it. So Geoffrey just stared blankly, hoping some invisible hand would reach out and smack him with purpose.

Eventually he got tired of doing nothing. He thought it was probably best to at least pretend he was being productive, and since he was hungry, he walked into his kitchen area to make something.

Now up and moving with a purpose, no matter how small, he was able to think marginally more clearly. "I should make something that requires effort, to keep me busy. The more I do, the more... alive I'll feel.

"And now you're talking to yourself. Lovely. Of course all the research suggests it's healthy, especially in this state of mind. Probably. I don't care enough to check, and I *am* feeling somewhat uplifted, so we'll go with that. Even if it's a placebo effect, it'll do." He looked in his refrigerator to examine his ingredients. "Something something something... that I can cook. Alright, I see bread, eggs, some turkey... pickles, olives— Oof, leftover chicken, two days has not been kind to you. I'll throw you out later. It is a little early, so perhaps a breakfast sandwich? That seems reasonably involved."

Geoffrey pulled out two eggs, the bag of sliced turkey, the ketchup bottle, and a bagel from a bag he found behind the bread. It all seemed to look and smell plenty fine, so he proceeded to crack the eggs into a pan and begin to scramble them. He sliced his bagel and put it in the toaster, setting it to 'two' to get it warm and just a bit dark. Once his eggs were done, he warmed the turkey in the pan briefly, and set it all on his bagel—with a small squirt of ketchup spread over one side—and sat down to eat, instinctively grabbing one of the newspapers from the counter.

He found himself looking at the front page of Thursday's newspaper, getting back into his normal routine.

"This is good." Geoffrey said to himself aloud. "This is progress, this is... recovery."

The front page naturally consisted of more articles regarding the hostage crisis orchestrated by Mayor Liu. This article did seem to focus more on the vigilante involved, though. Of course, it asked more questions than it answered; the hero had appeared from practically nowhere. He fought with some still-unexplained monster a week prior, then suddenly was called out by a group of kidnappers by order of the mayor. There was no more information beyond that. No sign of where he came from or disappeared to, no comment from Minh Liu or the police officers who arrested him with Shatterbug's evidence.

Geoffrey had little patience for blind speculation in his news sources, though, and so turned the pages of his New Jackson Republic in search of something more stimulating. It seemed not much else of import occurred in the past few days, locally anyway. He was about to get up to take a look at today's news, but something in this issue caught his eye just before he put it down.

He wasn't sure what about it had drawn him in. It was very plain, it had practically no information, and yet it was just vague enough to be intriguing—exciting, even.

PHYSICIST SEEKING ENGINEER FOR

LUCRATIVE COOPERATIVE PROJECT

Doctor Strauss knew many things. He knew how to build a machine to unlock the potential of the human mind, he knew how to lead a team of many different backgrounds, and he knew that when someone was this vague and yet also this transparent, they had something real.

Or perhaps that was his need for purpose which he now lacked, talking. Either way, he had nothing to lose, and was ever the optimist, even in the state he was in now, and so he resolved to call the attached phone number.

The line rang several times. He checked the number as he waited, ensuring he had entered it correctly. Again and again it rang, imploring him to wait, just wait, he'll answer in a moment, he hears it. He pulled the phone away from his ear at the seventh ring, and the screen flashed back on for him to press to hang up. Then the ring cut short, and he heard a faint voice come over the receiver.

"Hello? This is Marco Nieve."

Geoffrey quickly pulled the phone back to his ear. "Mister Nieve, my name is Doctor Strauss; I'm calling with regards to your advertisement in the Republic."

"Oh, oh wait— OH!" the voice exclaimed. "Yes, yes hello, good to meet you— I mean to speak with you— er, thank you for calling!"

He sounded young, younger than Geoffrey expected anyway. "You said you were seeking an engineer? What sort of project are you working on?"

"Well, ah— I'm sorry, I'm not really in a good place to get into it right now, and it's kind of a... low-key project, if you understand me. I'd like to meet you before I explain too much."

Geoffrey paused briefly, considering whether to proceed. "I understand. I do feel I need to ask though, if you're able: what sort of work would I be doing?"

The voice seemed to think for a moment before responding. "Examining the practical side of an existing system. Possibly reverse-engineering it. My discipline is largely theoretical; I need some assistance with the mechanical and electronic aspects."

"Is it just you? How are you being funded?"

"Yes, it is— and I'm sorry, I really don't have the time to explain any further right now. Is this a cell phone? I'll text you my address and we can work out when to meet, then I'll answer everything."

"I... see." Strauss said, with more than a little hesitation. "Okay then, I look forward to it, Mister Nieve."

"Thank you, me too Doctor Strauss."

He supposed that could have been much less helpful. The man—the boy, really—was quite awkward; he didn't seem at all prepared for this situation. Yet his responses seemed genuine, particularly the explanation of the project goals, veiled though it was. What had he stumbled into?

Geoffrey's phone buzzed with a text. The number he'd just called sent him an address, and asked if the next day at two in the afternoon worked for him. He replied that he would meet the boy there—in kinder words, of course. He opened up his contacts to program his new presumptive partner in. Marco Nieve. He would remember that name.

Issue 5
Saving the World

Marco could not imagine being more excited or anxious. Could this be the chance to get some answers, at last? He knew he wouldn't fully understand everything, but having a solid grasp of the suit was a bigger step in the right direction than he had been able to take so far on his own.

However, at the same time, he needed to be cautious in his hope that Strauss could be trusted, if he even wanted to be involved at all. There was a lot of risk here, but from the little research Marco was able to pull up on the doctor, he believed him to be a reasonable and trustworthy man. Of course, a few peer-reviewed papers and a simple note of employment with the government did not a good man make.

Marco spent several hours ensuring his dorm was organized and clean for his guest. He went back and forth several times on where to put the Shatterbug armor. Out in the open would make a statement, but was more dangerous if this man was not what he appeared. But if he kept it stowed away in a closet, and tried to ease his guest into things, there was a chance he'd walk out before even giving it a chance—or not believe him, in which case he'd reveal the suit, making its concealment moot anyway. In the end, he opted to lay it out on his coffee table. It was fitting, after all, that Doctor Strauss should learn about it where Marco first encountered it.

After cleaning up his microwave lunch, Marco turned to playing some more Terminus 2, killing time until his potential partner arrived. He had defeated Ophion last weekend, and was now going back to find secrets, finish sidequests, and ultimately just aim for absolute completion. He started the Ivory Tower questline some time ago, but never got around to actually devoting any effort into it. Now, with the main plot finished, he could invest himself in freeing the surrounding area from its curse.

The Ivory Tower was a unique way to implement a linear objective, the most interesting that Marco had experienced in gaming in a long time. Each quest had him ascend two or three levels in an effort to reach the top, only to stop short ahead of some obstacle that he could not surpass. He'd then have to climb back down and explore the world at large—engaging in other, unrelated sidequests, even—to find the weapons he needed to defeat the monster, or learn the tricks to solve the puzzles, and move on. It was effectively a more engaging fetch-quest, and Marco appreciated it.

He was in the middle of the sixth level of the Tower when, at 2:07 PM, Marco heard a knock on his door. As the New Jackson State University campus was itself a part of the city, there were really no safeguards to prevent non-students from entering campus housing areas. Electronic security sufficed, along with the blue light emergency system that had become the national standard, scattered about.

Marco paused his game and stood up to open the door. "Welcome, Doctor Strauss." he said before even registering his caller's appearance. Once he finished, he took in the man at his door. He wore a hoodie, which Marco found odd for a doctor. His pants were somewhat nice, if a little warm for the weather. His shoes gave away his maturity, being more appropriate than sneakers, but of course, they were by no means dressy. His hands were by his side, though they had extensive bandaging.

"Are you ok?" he asked instinctively, nodding his head to the wrappings.

"I'm fine; skin condition. Doctor Geoffrey Strauss." replied the man, extending his hand. Marco shook it firmly, though not to the degree he would have normally, so as not to hurt the doctor's skin. "May I come in?"

"Oh yes, of course." Marco stood aside as Geoffrey—Marco assumed he could call him that—entered, not looking around too much.

"I apologize for being a bit late; when I arrived I wasn't fully certain I had the right address, given..." Geoffrey stood facing Marco, his back to the dorm room and, therefore, to the suit sprawled out in the living area.

"Yeah, I uh— sorry about that. I was in class when you called and had to step out, I didn't have time to mention. I wasn't completely honest in the ad, partly because it's actually kind of expensive to do, and partly because I needed to be clear, but vague. It's a... delicate subject." He glanced at the armor behind Doctor Strauss. "I *am* a physics *student*—a good one. I just know that there's a certain stigma when someone hears that. I hope that won't be any trouble."

Strauss began to turn and fully enter the room.

"It's no trouble—at least, I should hope not. I just wasn't expecting it is all, I'm not too big on—" he stopped short as he saw the Shatterbug outfit before him. "Surprises."

There was a brief silence in the room, and the doctor was completely still. "Is that...?" Geoffrey finally said.

"Yeah, that's uh… that's why you're here."

"But—" he turned to face Marco again. "But then, you're—"

"Shatterbug. I am, yeah."

Strauss' eyes widened. At first, Marco was unsure whether it was out of fear, anger, excitement, or greed. He got his answer when the doctor turned and ran toward the suit, as if it was a present left out for him to unwrap. He set the duffel bag he had brought with him down on the couch, and kneeled at the coffee table, taking in the machine.

"Amazing; an armored suit capable of exerting such tremendous forces! I saw the phone-captured videos online, of course, but to see it with my own eyes… How does it work?"

"Well, that's largely why you're here: I'm not sure. I sort of inherited it. Oh, and it's not just a super-strength suit." Marco said, sitting down in the chair at the head of the suit.

Over the next several minutes, Marco explained what the suit actually did: how it split its wearer into three copies when prompted with a voice command, spread out in five-minute intervals in the past, present and future. How when they reconstitute, the act of time folding in on itself creates a force that emulates super strength. How they can reunite from any of the duplicates, allowing for travel forward or backward across five minutes of time. Marco did leave out, however, the exact means by which he obtained the suit, and his doppelganger's warning of the psychotic oncoming darkness. Through all of this, Geoffrey listened patiently and attentively, absorbing all of this information and glancing at the suit every so often, as if to ask for its secrets.

"Now, on to what I've learned," Marco continued, moving on from explanation to report. "Which is to say, very little. That cylinder in the chest cavity? It contains a sample of pure, one-hundred percent Element 120."

"But that's—"

"I know. There's wires hooked into the metal ends of the casing, which can be detached to remove it. This leads me to believe it acts as the power source for the suit, but I don't understand how. Additionally, under these plates are some seriously complicated electronics. There's motors and such implying some amount of motion is necessary for the time travel, but that kind of theoretical physics is way beyond me, especially when I really have no practical training with electronics or machines. That's where you come in, I hope."

"I see. Hm, well let me see here." Geoffrey replied, eagerly reaching into his bag in search of something. After a moment, he pulled out a small tool and—looking to Marco for permission—used it to pry the right breastplate off.

He got out some other tools, some simple, some electronics that Marco had no idea as to what they were or what they did. Doctor Strauss poked and prodded at various parts of the system beneath the plate, sometimes causing lights to flicker or motors to spin for a moment. He worked silently and methodically, taking care not to so much as scratch anything. Eventually he returned the plate to its original position, and moved on to another. Once again, he fiddled with the machinery beneath it with an assortment of tools, occasionally pulling a new one out of his bag. Marco was curious how he had come so prepared, but assumed these were simply standard electrician or engineer's tools; what did he know?

For about an hour, Marco waited patiently as Strauss painstakingly looked under every plate. Once he had, he went on to inspect the visor, though didn't spend much time there after acknowledging the microphone. Finally, he moved on to the glass window in the middle of the armor.

"You'll need forceps or something to spin the metal bit, that'll open it up." Marco helpfully informed his associate.

"Ah, very interesting." the doctor replied, with genuine awe. He did as instructed, sliding the glass casing out of the way and carefully removing the cylinder, keeping it close to the cavity so the cords could stay connected to the tube. He took a few of his tools to the ends of the wires where they met the metal, before unhooking them.

"May I?" he asked quietly, referring to removing the Element 120 from its container.

"Of course, yes." replied Marco with a whisper.

Strauss opened the glass cylinder and removed the sample carefully, caressing it in his gloved hands. He held it up to the light, then close to his eye, then cupped in his palms to simulate darkness. After measuring it, inspecting it with what looked to be a jeweler's loop, and reading it with another device retrieved from the duffel, he returned the sample to its case, and returned that to its compartment in the suit. He sat up on the couch, still looking at the armor.

"So," he began, a tone of excitement detectable in his voice. Marco sat forward, eager to hear the doctor's findings. "The electronics under the plates seem to behave like individual modules, many of them doing different things, but behaving as one machine for one purpose. Fortunately, for the most part, I understand what each of these modules it intended for, what they do."

Marco had to keep from jumping out of his seat at this.

"The problem is that, understanding this, I don't see any way that they could or should be creating the time distortion effect you've described. But, that's not what I'm most interested in."

Marco felt deflated for a moment, but perked up quickly with interest. "So what are you interested in?" he asked confusedly.

"The Element 120. Or more specifically, the cylindrical core on the whole. The sample you see there, it isn't the only one present. There are two more, very small pieces of it in either end of the casing."

"Why? What does that mean?"

"From what I can tell, it seems Element 120 has a very curious property. Rather than letting off a radiation field, it instead causes the things around it to vibrate very minutely, invisibly to the naked eye and only barely picked up by machines. But, when two independent samples are within each other's fields, this oscillation can be detected, and in fact is very powerful. The sample in the glass casing doesn't seem to do much here, like it's for show. The metal ends contain systems to collect the kinetic energy from the two smaller pieces causing one another to shake, and turn it into electrical energy. The visible one does so as well, but it's superficial in terms of power output. What's most interesting here, though, is that we can discern from the state of the display sample that the decay of the Element 120 due to this oscillation is unprecedentedly slow. It also doesn't seem to cause any damage to the materials around it. At least, not these materials, or organic materials obviously, like our skin."

"So I was right, it does power the suit." Marco said with interest and pride, but also some solemnity. This didn't explain how the suit worked, only how it got the energy to work.

"Yes, but you're missing my point. It will power this suit *indefinitely*. A battery this size could power, say, the entire city of New Jackson for longer than the Earth will be alive."

Marco's eyes widened. Now he understood the gravity of the situation. "So what do we do with this information?"

"Well that's obvious, Marco. We sell it."

"What?" he replied, his mouth agape. He nearly stood up in shock.

"What else? Power like this could revolutionize humankind as we know it. With more of this element, the entire world could have effective, infinite, clean energy."

"No; out of the question. The world needs Shatterbug, it needs this suit."

"I think you misunderstand me, Mister Nieve. I don't want to get rid of the suit or take this from you. I want to work with you. If we find more of this element— well, let me put it his way. Nearly all conflict in the modern world results from the control of one commodity: power. Oil, uranium, sunlight; nations vying for control of these resources is the root of nearly all strife on Earth. The unending struggle for funds to provide relief to those in need is undercut by a lust for more energy than is necessary to provide it. If the world had access to power like this, why, there would be no need for Shatterbug. With more of this Element 120, Marco, we can save the world."

Marco looked back in wonder. What would have happened if he had refused to work with Strauss on that day four months ago? How different would the world be? How different would he be? As he looked beside him, at his partner listening with him to the murmurs of the press out in front of the stage, he decided that thinking on it was silly. Whether anything would be better didn't matter, because he could always try to make this the best outcome.

It had been a long road leading here. Four months may not seem like a long time looking forward; it may not even look like a long time looking back, for most. However, when one had been as busy as Marco and Geoffrey had, when one had accomplished as much as them, it seemed eternal.

It did not take much more convincing on Doctor Strauss' part beyond that impressive speech to get the heroic part of Marco on board, but his realistic side—his worried and anxious side—held back, kicking and screaming, for weeks.

The first step was trying to see if more 'Element 120' even existed. That took a lot of strong letters, long phone calls, and shameless groveling to get started on. Finally, one of Geoffrey's old government contacts was willing to respond, and while he could not make the unilateral decision to help them, he was able to give the duo a foot in the door. After they were able to provide evidence of the discovery—and its applications, though still keeping Shatterbug close to the chest—they were permitted a very brief, supervised utilization of NASA's existing Earth Observing System satellites to search for signs of the element, deep within the Earth.

Marco wasn't sure how they had gotten so lucky where others had failed, but they discovered a large vein of Element 120 buried in the crust underneath the Arctic Ocean, stretching completely underwater; with the exception of a few small peninsulas on the northwest coast of Greenland. He chalked it up to the fact they had used the system in a way that it was not intended, and therefore in a way that was not attempted, but that it was capable of regardless. The as-of-then nonexistent corporation of Marco and Geoffrey's struck deals almost immediately, with the U.S. Department of Defense offering grants and funding for their private acquisition of the vein.

The paperwork took a few weeks to file and finalize, but once everything fell into place, Marco Nieve became Chief Executive Officer and co-founder of Snow Dynamics Enterprises, with Doctor Geoffrey Strauss as the Chief Operating Officer. Some clever loopholes needed to be found and taken advantage of, however, as Strauss was still technically blacklisted from government funding until the completion of his project's investigation—although his personal involvement had been ruled out. But, so long as he was simply an employee of the company— even an executive one—and not an owner or shareholder, he was technically not a recipient of the grants. It was therefore decided that the company would not be publicly traded. Government funding took care of the major cost of the land anyway, and once they had that, Geoffrey's exceptional credit score and notoriety as a peer-reviewed engineer afforded them bank loans to cover initial mining and facilities costs.

Once the mining operation was underway, the two partners began looking into ways to utilize the vibrating batteries. As part of the deal with the Department of Defense, they had to put a certain degree of research and development into military and defense applications of the energy source. Both Geoffrey and Marco, however, were adamant that their company would not be in the business of weapons manufacturing. Communications, non-military vehicles, and energy supplies for public consumption were all acceptable though, and these were the first fields of research that prototyping took place in.

The Snow Dynamics office was, at first, one large, plain building. A few offices attached to one reasonably sized workshop, with a staff of only ten. They saved a lot on energy by hooking their own batteries into the structure's wiring, disconnecting completely from the city grid. They only needed to produce prototypes, though, as once the Defense Department signed off on them, they were able to rent assembly space for mass production, until they could afford their own plants. This research and development accelerated and produced results at an impressive rate; a testament to the versatility of the Element 120. Given that, and how little was required for the batteries, only seven weeks passed before their first private manufacturing plant came into operation.

As pre-celebration on the eve of the conference they were now waiting to speak at, Marco and Geoffrey treated their small staff to a night at the bar. They had rented the Quiver Arcade Bar out of their own pockets, knowing it was often frequented by a number of their employees, and even Marco on occasion.

It was a night of drinking, video gaming, and team building. Although he was old enough to drink, Marco was not partial to alcohol himself. In college, he would often be gently teased for this aversion, but tonight it made him a hero: the designated driver.

He was the youngest attendee, and definitely had better hand-eye coordination than his competition, but when it came to the classic game consoles, the others had much more experience. He was knocked out of the Space Invaders tournament in the first round, left to cheer on Geoffrey, who easily cleaned up the contest. He made it to the finals of the Pac Man bracket, but was beat out by the computer-like strategy of Michelle Ramirez.

By the end of the night, most everyone was winding down, resigning to sitting at the tables, drinking beer and eating appetizers, determined to keep the party going. Marco and Geoffrey sat together, and as one of the technicians walked off to the restroom, the CEO thought it a good time to relish with his friend in their triumph.

"Having a good time, Geoff?" he asked the doctor, who had claimed earlier could hold his liquor.

"Yes, very. It's lovely seeing everyone so excited." Strauss slurred, just past the beginning of intoxication.

"They should be. We all should be, we've done so much, and we're going to be able to do so much more."

Geoffrey burped quietly to himself. "Excuse me!"

The two laughed with each other, like they had shared a clever joke, before he continued. "What do you want to do?"

"I dunno." he shrugged. "We can sit here and eat some more, maybe try and start another contest in a few minutes. I think I can beat these geezers at Asteroids, especially now that they've all had a few–"

"No, Marco. I mean—" he hiccuped, the heavy drafts slowly catching up with him. "I mean, what do you want to do with the company, now that we're going public? Now that you're going public?"

"Oh, I gotcha." He thought hard on this. The obvious answer was what they had decided on together, four months ago: saving the world. Supplying clean energy to everyone, finding new ways to improve human life. But, Marco knew his friend was trying to look deeper than that. "I suppose, I want to learn more about the suit. With the new resources, a new office, more staff, we might be able to understand why it does it what does. Where it came from."

"Where it came from?" Strauss pried, dropping another fry into his mouth. Marco still had yet to explain the origins of the suit; what little he knew, anyway.

"Yeah, the person who gave it to me—who I inherited it from—he never really said where he got it. Just that it was given to him in a similar way."

"Who was he?" The doctor seemed to ease out of his dip into drunkenness with the stimulating conversation.

"Doesn't matter." Marco replied, grimly. "He's dead. And he wasn't anyone important when he was alive."

"A shame." Geoffrey paused for a long time, then raised his glass in Marco's direction.

"What are we toasting?" he asked with confusion, raising his own glass of soda slowly.

"You. To Marco!" shouted the doctor, attracting the attention of the assembled partygoers. "That he may be a greater man than we deserve, a greater hero than we need."

"And to Geoff!" Marco interjected, before anyone could complete the toast. "Without whom, I would never have learned what being a great man meant, and what being a hero felt like."

"Here here!" the bar sounded. All in attendance clinked their plastic glasses and glass bottles in celebration.

Back in the present, however, Marco saw his cue from the other side of the stage, snapping him out of his memories and indicating that he and Geoffrey were ready to meet the public of New Jackson, and the world.

He stepped out in front of the podium, readying himself.

"Good morning, New Jackson. My name is Marco Nieve; you have not heard of me." he began, reciting from memory, though checking his script in front of him occasionally, if only to stay on pace and not trip over his words in excitement. "My partner, Doctor Geoffrey Strauss, you perhaps may have heard of. But, we are not here because of who you did or didn't know us as. We are here to share with you what we will come to be known as. I have several announcements for you, so let's begin by getting the big one out of the way.

"I, Marco Nieve, am the vigilante known as Shatterbug." Marco gestured for the suit to be carted on stage for the cameras to all see. "The Shatterbug armor that you see here was a gift to me. And while I intend to continue to take the mantle as a hero within the law, that is not why you're here, either."

The crowd immediately lit up with shouted questions, flashing cameras, and raised hands. Marco expected this, but he was not prepared for the barrage that was the real thing. He waved his hands for everyone to relax so that he could continue.

"The Shatterbug suit is powered by a small battery, constructed using samples of Element 120; an element that up until now has been purely theoretical, undiscovered in nature and unsynthesized in laboratories. It is capable of producing near infinite, clean energy, with unbelievable efficiency; and we have more. We are announcing that Doctor Strauss and I have started Snow Dynamics Enterprises, dedicated not only to the safe research of this element and its public and private applications, but to the production and distribution of its clean power across the world, *at cost.* We want the world to glow with inexpensive, reliable energy, to rescue us from endless conflict over oil and nuclear power. Element 120—or as we have come to call it, *marconium*—is completely harmless, produces no waste, and can yield electricity with effectively no supervision. This leads me to my next announcement.

"While marconium itself is safe, just as anything else, it can be utilized for harm. For this reason, to prevent the misuse of marconium in any capacity, Snow Dynamics has seized ownership of its sole naturally occurring vein, and with government approval, is to be responsible for oversight of all research, care, and development of the element and its related technologies as they are developed. This is to ensure the term 'marconium bomb' and things of the like are never, ever coined."

Again, the crowd of reporters roared with questions and demands. Marco tried to continue speaking over the mumbling and occasional shouts of the assembled media, in an effort to calm them and stay on message.

"We have every intention of total transparency as to the projects we are working on, to ensure that nothing is produced that isn't inherently beneficial to the world at large. Furthermore, we will be launching a serious corporate outreach program starting in two weeks, to assist current energy providers who opt into the program in transitioning to marconium power cells, under the stipulations that they reduce the costs to their consumers, and put more focus into developing and maintaining their power grids. We pledge to be dedicated to total—"

Screams from the crowd interrupted Marco, now. He thought he was doing well with politely continuing over the frustratingly impatient reporters, but apparently not. Either way, he was not expecting any screams, so he turned to his partner for support before continuing. When he did turn back, however, he realized that his speech did not cause the screaming.

Geoffrey Strauss had been shot.

There was a bullet wound in his chest, and blood staining his white shirt and grey jacket. The doctor looked to his friend and partner in horror before trying to grab onto his shoulder for balance. He missed, and Marco failed to catch him as a number of the venue's security personnel rushed on stage, some practically dragging Marco away while the others attempted to tend to Strauss.

The hall was chaos. Marco tried to look back to find Geoffrey and make sure he was okay, but he lost sight of him. It wasn't even clear whether he was still on the stage or had been pulled away as well. In fact, nothing was clear. People were running and screaming all around him. A few enterprising reporters and camera workers started or continued to document the events, but Marco was unable to hear them or even make out the words from their lips. He was in sensory overload and emotional turmoil.

Eventually he was outside, waiting as policemen canvassed the area, searching every person for weapons. He couldn't tell if they were having any success, and the officer who took Marco's statement wasn't eager to offer anything in return. Luckily, they returned the Shatterbug suit to him, and he packed it back away hurriedly into a briefcase.

"Damnit, I should have worn it! I knew I should have worn it, shown them what it really did!" he cursed to himself. Geoffrey had convinced him it wasn't necessary; after all, he said, it wasn't even clear to him, knowing and believing what it did, that Marco was doing anything when he shattershocked or reconstituted.

Finally, the detective in charge approached him to bring him up to speed.

"We haven't found the weapon or the shooter. Given the small space and the lack of any bullet casings, we believe it was a single-shot handgun; easily concealed or disposed of. We'll continue looking for any information we can once forensics gets back with info from the recordings."

"Where's Doctor Strauss? Did he make it?" Marco asked anxiously. He was concerned, not for his company or even his partner, but for his friend.

"We're not certain. He seems to have disappeared. There's a trail of blood leading off the stage, but it stops behind the curtain, like he was picked up. No blood after that would seem to indicate his wound was covered, so we can assume he was still alive when he vanished."

"But, then— he was kidnapped?" he asked with confusion and anger.

"That is how we're treating the situation for the moment; likely a targeted attack, but it's unclear whether it was a failed assassination or a successful abduction. We will keep you updated, but please call us if you think of any more information that might help in finding him." The detective handed Marco a card. "Oh, and I'd recommend not taking this into your own hands. This is much more serious than what you dealt with back in January; and from the sounds of it, you're more than just a vigilante now."

Marco sighed with the weight of the situation. With or without the suit, he felt more helpless and less informed now than he had in a long time.

Issue 6
Null Hypotheses

"This office is really flippin' cold." Marco said aloud, though as more of a general grumble than a serious complaint. "I know it's ninety degrees outside but *Dios mio*, there's such a thing as overcompensating!"

The new Snow Dynamics Enterprises corporate headquarters stood at the northern end of the downtown area of New Jackson, right along Central Avenue. At twenty-four stories, it was only a little more than half the size of the tallest building in the city, but it was the tallest in the immediate area and therefore commanded attention. Of course, it wasn't built in a month; it had already existed, but stood mostly empty for several years when the real estate fell through. Marco and Doctor Strauss were able to acquire it only a week and a half before their press release, and planned to begin relocation there in the weeks following, after the electrical system had been refitted to run on marconium power.

There it was again. Marco caught himself thinking about Geoffrey far too often. This was just as much his company as it was Marco's, maybe even more. He certainly contributed more to the day-to-day activities as COO. Or had done, anyway.

Even after a month, the authorities had no information of Strauss' whereabouts, or even confirmation of life. There was never a ransom, never a threat of anything further. All they wanted was Geoffrey, and they didn't care to explain why.

Despite warnings, of course, Marco did try to investigate himself. Five minutes of time only got one so much, though; there were simply no leads to follow. And when most abduction cases go cold after only forty-eight hours, this was one instance that time was not on his side.

So he tried to bury himself in his work—their work. As much as he wanted to keep the Chief Operating Officer's seat open for Strauss when he did turn up, it simply wasn't feasible. Marco promoted one of the first employees they had hired together to fill the role: Michelle Ramirez. An exceptional engineer and team player, Ms. Ramirez had more experience than anyone else in the company, besides Doctor Strauss. There was simply no contest.

Much of Snow Dynamics' work was still focused on prototyping at the moment; coming up with new projects to experiment with using the versatile marconium being mined in the Arctic Circle. Of course, Michelle wasn't the only one getting anything done. There were dozens of new employees for Marco to oversee, and while he wasn't able to personally interact with all of them—though he would like to get around to doing so—he was responsible for determining the direction of their research and approving new developments, overseeing not only the corporate offices, but also the new manufacturing plant and the mining expedition, when they required his attention. Naturally, all of this meant college was no longer an option; in fact he had dropped out when their first grant was approved and it was clear he and Geoffrey would be going places, almost three months ago.

Today's itinerary was a bit dry on the CEO's end. Yesterday, Marco led another follow-up conference call with the board of directors of the New Jackson Public Service Company, the largest electric utility in the state. He was largely just waiting to hear back from them.

They were being much more difficult than Marco had anticipated regarding Snow Dynamics' OmniGrid program, an effort to work with power providers in becoming marconium-fueled services. It was designed to reduce costs for the energy company, under the agreement that costs would also be reduced for their consumers, with money that would have gone into maintaining less efficient energy supply systems being diverted into maintaining the power grid itself, bringing more efficient, clean energy to more homes and businesses.

Of course, once corporate bigwigs hear 'price drops' and 'regulations,' they try to negotiate out of them in any way they can. Fortunately, Marco was young and stubborn, plus he had the support of the public. He knew things would work out.

It was around lunch time, and so he decided to walk out to the reception area of the executive floor and ask the secretary, Branden, to order some food. He could have paged Branden, of course, but he didn't like using the phone for things he was able to walk to, especially for things as trivial as asking for take-out.

Marco considered what he wanted as he walked out the door from his office, but upon stepping to the other side he found himself... somewhere else.

He was still in the same building; the layout was the same, though the remodelling the company had done was not there, and there were no desks, or phones, or people. It was an empty floor; an empty building.

"Mister Nieve." a voice spoke confidently from behind him. It was definitely male, but it sounded more impressive than a simple man's voice. He turned back into what should have been his office, which now instead of a desk, a seating area, and some counter space, contained only a man, though he was not quite plain enough to be a man.

Or rather, the man looked plain enough. He was tall, and probably would have been called lanky were he not just a little too heavy for the title. He wore a long, grey, woolen cloak with a high collar, though it was down and professional. It was buttoned up completely, but the shirt underneath seemed to be a lighter grey, though only just, with the jacket between the two a much darker shade. As much of the legs that Marco could see wore pants matching the jacket beneath the long coat, and his shoes were a polished black. By all accounts, his face, his hair, his eyes, were all aggressively plain. Yet he still felt indescribably impressive and unique.

"Who's asking?" Marco replied, unsure of how to proceed.

"I am not asking. You are Marco Nieve. You are Shatterbug." His voice didn't sound as Marco had expected. With how he looked, and the aura he gave off, he expected something superior. English, maybe, or even more foreign and unique. Instead, the man had no accent at all, no interesting quirks of the tongue or unusual stresses of some sounds. It was an uninteresting voice, and that made it curiously impressive.

"And you are?" He thought it best not to confirm or deny the man's statements just yet.

"I am called Null. And in the interest of ending this confused not-quite interrogation, you are in my parallel to your Snow Dynamics Enterprises." the plain man affirmed.

"Your parallel? I'm going to need a little more information."

The peculiar man called Null didn't respond immediately as he had up until now. Marco wasn't sure he would for a moment. After a few seconds, however, he spoke up. "Of course. My apologies. I've not interacted with someone I respect in some time."

Marco thought to press him on this, but as the man was proceeding anyway, he decided against it.

"I created this universe. It is a parallel to ours; a copy, identical in every way with the exception that time here runs a few months ahead of the original. I designed it to watch over our home world without needing to directly interact with it, however some... inconsistencies have begun to develop, and they threaten my system. I wish to understand this, and if necessary, protect the original universe."

The information Null was providing would be helpful, Marco imagined, if it weren't so rapid and incomplete.

"You... created this place? What are you, some kind of god?" was all he could think to ask, to start with anyway.

The man pulled one of his hands out from his coat pocket, revealing a white velvet glove and a silver pocket watch. Null glanced at it briefly before returning it and his gloved hand to his pocket. "In this instance, I recognize you will require more details, and I am inclined to provide them. But not here." He nodded his head as invitation for Marco to turn around. As he did so, he once again found himself in his office, the door closed. Turning back around, he saw Null standing in front of one of the couches of the sitting area.

"Inform Branden that you will be in a telephone meeting, and that you cannot be disturbed. Then I will explain my actions."

Marco still wasn't sure what this was. His mind was racing, asking questions of himself in an attempt to try to guess and figure out what this Null person was and why he was here. Was this the darkness he had been warned about? Or was this meant to be some recruitment, some way to gather allies who knew more than him in order to fight the darkness? Marco knew one thing: he was confident either way. Ever since the press conference, he had taken to wearing the Shatterbug outfit at all times, his visor off and folded back, and the armor concealed beneath his clothes. It was a bit uncomfortable in business suits, of course, but he got used to it. It was safer this way.

He turned back to his office door once more, poking his head out to relay the message to the secretary. After closing the door again, he walked back to his desk, and Null began.

"I am from this universe. I was born here, a human on Earth, and I assume led an ordinary life here. Seven months ago, an event occurred. In all my investigations I have yet to determine exactly what this event was, or the cause of it, but I believe it resulted in whoever I was being lost. Very little was left behind, and it is this that I have gathered, along with what I have made for myself, to become Null.

"What was also left behind was an ability." The grey-clothed man pulled his hands out of his pockets, revealing their plain white gloves once more. He twisted them about each other in front of him; the motions would look to be the casting of a spell, if something weren't happening with each gesture.

First, he pressed his closed fists together by the knuckles of his thumbs. He pulled his hands apart, and a gold-colored reflective cylinder emerged, as if he had been holding it in his hands the whole time. Once it had reached a length of about a foot, he held it up in one hand, using the other to pinch some point in the middle of the rod. Although there should have been nothing to pull on, the bar began to unroll itself into a flat sheet of reflective metal. He did this until his hands held a square sheet of the material, then began to fold it. One would mistake it for origami, were the sheet folding in simple linear creases. Rather, it was becoming something much more complicated and intricate. Finishing this shaping, Null again pinched at a portion of the fabrication which should not have had anything to hold onto, pulling out another stem and bending it slightly as he did so. He pinched two asymmetrical leaves from the new shape, and set it down on Marco's desk for him to inspect.

Right before his eyes, Null had fashioned a metal rose out of nothing at all.

"I can create, I have found, any type of matter, such as brass, and fashion it into whatever I like. This skill seems dependent only on my knowledge and physical limitations; the matter and energy is derived from nowhere."

"That's not possible. Nothing can create matter, it must be coming from somewhere!" interjected Marco, unable to help himself.

"Perhaps it is, I have yet to find its source if so; but that is not the point. So long as I understand what I am creating, it exists. Some things need perfect knowledge, like machines. A copy of a universe, apparently, only requires a general understanding of the laws of physics of that universe. I therefore did this, for fear of bringing any harm to this world as I learned to understand myself. I desynchronized the two worlds so as to keep an eye on the original.

"The problem I come to you now for began seven months ago, or more accurately, the equivalent of that time in my own world. In my duplicate world, the event which created me did not occur. At first I thought this odd, but not terribly surprising; perhaps my lack of understanding of certain concepts—or even a subconscious understanding of others—prevented another Null from being created.

"But then, the equivalent of five months ago, I noticed another discrepancy. You."

"Is... is my doppelganger missing?" For a moment, Marco believed he had learned where the suit may have come from. This would explain so much: how there was a second Marco, why Null's world didn't seem to have a Snow Dynamics. Everything was starting to make sense in Marco's head, all of the questions he was—

"No, your 'doppelganger' is safe and accounted for."

So much for learning the secrets of the Shatterbug suit.

"The problem with you, Marco," Null continued, "is that the version of you in my world did not become Shatterbug. The suit was not gifted to him by another Marco, Julio Carillo never became Titan Black, Mayor Liu was never arrested, and Marco Nieve and Geoffrey Strauss never started Snow Dynamics Enterprises. Something has caused our two universes, which should be perfect duplicates, to diverge. Something in this world is unique, it cannot be duplicated or accounted for. It seems to involve you, in more ways than one, but I believe it originated seven months ago, when I became Null."

"So you need my help to figure out why our two worlds are different, and you chose me because I'm the part that's different?"

"I want your help because you are a hero. I believe you will do important things in the future, and I wish to aid you in that. But in order to do so effectively, I need to have my early warning system back in place."

Marco always worried that he was too trusting of people. He was always skeptical, of course, internally, and he never found himself regretting letting someone in, but it was always a flaw he saw in himself. He was concerned that one day, that perceived flaw would be confirmed, and now here, with Null, that concern was at its strongest. The stakes were high, the knowledge was scarce or uncharted, and though he didn't like to admit it, Marco was still new when it came to being Shatterbug.

A healthy amount of skepticism goes a long way, but with this offer standing in front of him, he didn't feel like he had the luxury of time to consider and research.

"What would you need me to do?" he finally asked, still not fully committing.

"For the moment, help me look for clues to the source of the discrepancy. In my findings, I have learned of three other incidents which occurred on the same day as my event. They seem insignificant—they were merely accidents and only one person was killed at each, none of whom are of any relevance in my world—but there, the accidents did not occur, and they survived. Whether it is related to my creation or to your suit remains to be seen, but even if they are not, they may provide insight into what is responsible."

Still, Marco was unsure. Technically, Null's problem didn't directly affect him. It was a problem in the copy universe, and therefore not his responsibility.

Although, even he could see the implications that something had been manipulating events in this world, in his life, for some time. Even if they couldn't resolve Null's world's symmetry with this one, they may stumble upon information about Marco's 'mission' or the origins of the Shatterbug armor.

"Where do we start?" Marco said, giving in. He would go with Null, tentatively for now, in the hopes of getting the answers that had eluded him for nearly half a year.

Marco blinked.

When he opened his eyes, Null was standing in front of him, but they were somewhere else, now. Somewhere that didn't have a chair underneath him.

He fell.

When he got up, Marco looked around. They were standing in a train yard which seemed apparently ordinary. Men were working on loading pallets onto freight wagons, and a ways down he could see that a train had just left. On one of the cars nearby, not attached to a locomotive, he could see the logo for the New Jackson Railway Shipping Company.

"How are you teleporting us, by the way? I thought you only created things?" he asked.

"I can create portals from one point in space to another. It's very complicated metaphysics; I won't go into the details. But, I create them such that they exist only for a moment. Thus, it seems like teleportation. That's how I knew your world was beginning to diverge from mine; I open windows between the two from time to time."

That was good enough for Marco. He wasn't quite ready for another lecture.

"Seven months ago" Null began, lecturing Marco again, though not looking at him. "There was a serious explosion at this train yard. As I said, one person was killed, and while there was considerable property damage, they have been able to rebuild. However, this incident never happened in my duplicate world. How do you suggest we begin?"

"You're asking me? I thought you had this all planned?"

"I didn't ask for your assistance to string you along, Mister Nieve. You have a rapport with the people of this world; they won't be so willing to answer questions from me."

"Not everything belongs to my company, Null. I don't have any pull here."

"I am not telling you to be the CEO of Snow Dynamics Enterprises. I'm telling you to be Shatterbug."

Marco grumbled. His heroic persona was not some costume to put on for show or to get what he wanted. It was supposed to be used responsibly, to protect people and fight real threats. At least, that was what he wanted to do with it.

"Let's start slow. We'll find the manager on duty and see what he can tell us."

The two men in out-of-place clothes walked over to the group of workers transferring pallets from the train. "Excuse us, could you point my associate and I to your manager?" asked Marco.

One of the workers, a slender woman with her hair tied back, pulled a radio from her belt, only glancing at Marco. He was a little annoyed at this, but Null seemed ambivalent, and Marco couldn't argue that they were interrupting her. "Seven-oh-four to one-ten." she spoke into the receiver.

"Go for one-ten." the radio barked back shortly.

"I've got some men in suits by wagon twelve asking for you." she replied, again only briefly looking at them in her peripheral vision.

"Did they say who they're with?"

"Who are you guys?" she asked of them, now interested enough to directly acknowledge them.

"I'm Marco Nieve, with Snow Dynamics Enterprises." he replied.

"He's also known as Shatterbug." Null added, to Marco's minor annoyance.

The woman seemed unimpressed, and simply replied into the radio. "The superhero from Snow Dynamics."

"Copy," the radio began to respond. "Send him to the receiving office."

The woman pointed them to the main structure, directing them to turn left upon entering from the door on this side. Marco tried to thank her, but she was no longer inclined to pay them any mind, returning to her coworkers and the pallet of crates.

The two men entered the building and turned left to find themselves in a room that looked just a bit too small to be an office. There was an open garage door on the other end, like the room was intended to be a truck loading bay. One modest desk sat against the left wall, with one computer. Boxes were on three dolleys scattered around the room. The man in the desk turned at their entry to greet them.

"Hi, I'm Leonard Mullins, the receiving manager and M-O-D today. What can I help you with?" he said politely, though clearly confused as to why the CEO of a completely unrelated company was visiting him.

"Mister Mullins, my colleague and I were interested in the incident which occurred here last November." Marco offered.

"Whad'ya need to know?" he asked, again with a helpful but curious tone.

"Well, what exactly happened?"

"You must not watch the news much, Mister Nieve; it was all pretty cut-and-dry. One of my forklift operators, Vince Tripoli, was unloading some material—don't remember exactly what now, but it was something prone to explode. The containers were very safe, fail-safes and everything, and the other guys around said he was going perfectly by the book, moving slow. Hadn't even set it down yet when it popped. Forklift, the whole back end of that train, and most of the other half of this building were destroyed. And of course, Vince didn't make it. Poor guy was practically vaporized in the blast."

"You don't seem particularly upset." Null observed.

"It was months ago, and the company provided grief counseling; we've all learned to cope and move on. And as you can see, we've built back the damage, too." Mullins replied with the appearance of confidence, but clearly holding in some minor solemnity. "Why do you need to know about all this?"

"We suspect something may have been tampered with by an unknown party." Marco said quickly, trying to come up with a reasonable excuse for that, too. "I think it might be related to some other threats I've come across since becoming a hero. You mentioned that Mister Tripoli was operating the vehicle safely, yet the load still exploded. Was there ever any conclusion as to why that was?"

That was good enough for Mullins.

"Not really. No one wanted to come forward with anything. Liability and all." There was annoyance in his voice at that last notion, but he continued anyway. "The company who owned the material and was having it shipped claimed it wasn't volatile enough to produce an explosion like that without an intentional ignition, and the manufacturer that designed the storage units said there was no way they could have failed and let out any of the material or even allowed an internal explosion to get out of the containers. And as I said, New Jackson Rails couldn't be at fault because Vince was following every protocol to the letter. Of course, no one wanted to charge anyone else any fees for the accident. Everyone just decided to forget it even happened."

Leonard finished quietly. He was clearly still bothered by the situation's nonexistent closure.

"I see," Marco began after a moment. "Thank you, Mister Mullins. If you don't mind, we'd like to look at where it happened."

"I suppose I can show you around real quick, but there's not much to see. Like I said, we rebuilt just about everything that was lost and cleaned up the rest."

"That's alright; we'd still like to see it."

Mullins logged out of his computer and led the way outside, turning left and around to the other side of the building. They walked a little ways over to some tracks which were currently unoccupied.

He was right; Marco didn't see any trace of what had happened. There weren't even any scorch marks on the ground anymore. He supposed it would be too lucky to find something useful after so long.

"And you have no idea what the material was?" Null asked their guide.

"Not off the top of my head. What it was was the least of my problems that day; it wasn't even my load to receive, so I didn't have the paperwork."

"Would you be able to find the paperwork for us?" requested Marco, humbly.

"Not easily; it was last calendar year, all those reports were shipped off to corporate in January. You could talk to them, but given the circumstances, they may not want to be as compliant as me."

It seemed a dead end. There was no evidence of the incident or any specifics of the cause.

"Well, should we move on?" Marco asked, turning to Null.

"I think that would be best. The answers we need are not going to be found here." the man in grey declared.

Marco blinked.

He expected to be elsewhere again, but his eyes opened out of surprise, as Null's must have been too, because they still stood in the train yard. Marco had heard a loud crashing sound from behind him, and he turned on his heels to find the source.

On the horizon, the faint smoggy outline of downtown New Jackson was partially obscured by a ball of smoke and fire billowing upwards.

Marco turned to Null. "Visor on." he said firmly, indicating to his ally that they needed to go help. Null nodded in silent understanding.

Marco blinked.

When his eyes opened, the two men stood in the middle of a three-way intersection, just on the edge of the downtown area. Cars on all three adjoining roads were stopped and abandoned. Most were buckled inward, but a good number were on fire or totally exploded, reduced to ash and debris.

A few bodies were strewn about as well. Some were burned, some piles of sticky blood, totally liquefied and charred, and some were... frozen?

Unmistakably, there was ice on the roads and cars, covering even a few unfortunate souls, as if a freezing wind had blown through with intense force and prejudice, halting their escape. But how was that possible? It was the middle of summer in the New Jackson valley.

Marco quickly got his answer. Moving slowly down the road just ahead of him was the shape of a man, his arms outstretched and releasing blasts of visibly cold energy from his hands. Layers of ice formed on the metal of the cars in front of him, and the road beneath him became slippery, prompting him to walk carefully while also causing others to struggle in their attempt to flee.

"Shattershock!" Marco barked to his suit. The plates across his body shook with power and the marconium core warmed his chest, as his time-strewn copies' sights became visible within his visor.

All three Shatterbugs began their pursuit of the cold-emitting person down the road. Naturally, the past Marco reached him first, and with a resounding "Reconstitute!" the three duplicates were pulled backward in time, merging in the past as their united fist slammed into the villain, sending him forward before he even realized what happened. He slid across the ice and into one of the abandoned cars, giving the still lingering pedestrians a safe method of escape.

He stood up quickly, angered and surprised. He turned to face his assailant, scowling with rage as he clapped his hands together.

A vertical wave of freezing power began to expand and rush towards Marco. "Shattershock!" he yelled, with the intention of reconstituting in the future so as to avoid the blast. Before he was able to gather himself to do so, a silvery crystalline wall slid in front of him from his left, shielding him from the cold air. He looked to his left to see Null, apparently in the position from which he had sent the wall sliding towards Marco to protect him.

"Fight!" the otherworldly man shouted. "I'll rebuild the damage and add new pieces in your favor! Go!"

Marco was more than happy to comply with that. All three of him rushed towards the freezing man, tapping cars as they passed them to maintain their balance on the ice.

He got so used to running along the ice that when it melted in the future, seemingly instantly, he fell forward into the asphalt.

Future Marco got up quickly now, the rushing shallow water doing little to slow him. He looked all around for explanation, finding the source of the heat wave behind him: another mysterious man.

He extended his hands now, and a rush of air so impossibly hot that it was visibly charged was released, expanding outward more fiercely than the colder counterpart.

"Reconstitute!" shouted the Marco in the present, sending Shatterbug back and out of the way of the attack. But, he was still facing off against two super-powered individuals.

"Shattershock!"

Shatterbug looked around to confirm that the second figure was approaching from behind him, noting his partner's circumstance.

Both of the men reached a single arm towards him now, sending opposing forces of hot and cold energy out, threatening to converge on Marco. Again, a crystalline shield came to his aid, surrounding him like a bubble. The two forces met around and over the surface Null had constructed, resulting in a swirling dust devil and two very angry people.

"Who are you? What are you doing; what do you want?!" shouted Shatterbug from within the bubble, hoping they could hear him through whatever material Null had built it from.

He didn't get an answer right away. Instead, the shield began to glow, and Marco realized that some beam of energy was being directed at it from opposite Null. He was surrounded on all sides; the freezing man ahead of him, the boiling one behind, Null to his left, and this new power on the right. The shield began to become excited as the supercharged particles being shot at it bounced around, heating up the interior and Marco before the whole structure shattered.

He turned to face where the light had originated from to find a woman in torn and ragged clothes. Her hands were glowing, as were her eyes, with a white fury. He now noticed, in this brief moment of respite, that the two men were also in sore shape, and glowed with the same concerning power.

"We're the Disaster Pact, bug boy." the woman answered. "I'm Reactor. That's Iceberg, and that's Furnace. We're here to destroy."

"Destroy what? Explain your goals." Null commanded.

"To you? No." She launched her hand out in Marco's direction, past him and directly at the man in grey. He reached down to the ground and pulled up just in time, forming a wall of what had the appearance of acoustic paneling, refracting the oncoming light and dispersing it harmlessly.

Reactor looked shocked but unwavering. She nodded to Iceberg and Furnace, indicating that they should focus on destroying the one who creates.

Marco ran towards Reactor himself, who again attempted to send a stream of energy towards the hero. He reconstituted into the past, immediately shattershocking once more upon his arrival. His present self clenched his fist in preparation for his attack, but was shoved aside by the formation of another crystalline wall.

Shatterbug looked back to see a wave of heat pass over the wall and scald Reactor. In this moment of time, Null had yet to be attacked by the other two, and therefore was continuing to help Marco. He thought it time to return the favor.

"Reconstitute!" Shatterbug sent himself into the future, back to when Null was defending himself from all three villains.

"Null, what's going on?!" he shouted in the confusion, as attack after attack was launched at Null, whose actions became more desperate with each moment.

95

"I believe— eurf! I believe these three are the people who were meant to have died in the accidents! That one—the fiery one—he looks precisely like the Vince Tripoli living in my universe!"

"We did die!" Furnace interjected furiously. "Hyah!"

"We were brought back to life and granted these powers!" added Iceberg.

"To bring about the destruction of everything." Reactor finished. "So matter is created, it must be destroyed. We are that law, incarnate."

"That is not how reality works. Believe me." refuted Null as he created a steep pyramid of crystal beneath himself, lifting him up and forcing the others to all slide to the ground and away.

Of course Reactor only saw this as an opportunity, lighting it up with her light and sending the energy up and through the excited pyramid, hitting Null with all of her energy.

"Shattershock!" Marco shouted in a rage, sprinting towards the three villains. Iceberg and Furnace responded in kind, releasing wave after wave of their respective powers to keep Shatterbug at bay. The future Marco reconstituted out of the way, immediately shattershocking once more.

Again, the two wielders of temperature attacked the approaching hero, but his version in the present reconstituted to dodge them through time, as he continued his charge for Reactor. He shattershocked one final time and again travelled back into the past, out of the time of Iceberg and Furnace's waves. As one man, he grabbed hold of the wielder of light and thrust her into the ground.

Marco wasn't sure what came over him. In this short period of time, he had developed a connection, he thought, with Null. Therefore, seeing these three superpowered people attacking him so completely, ready to murder him so brutally, he momentarily lost control of his emotions.

He shattershocked, and once his past and future selves had rendered Reactor defenseless, they each began to pummel into her with undue hatred.

Null created two crystalline prisons to briefly hold the others, then set his hand onto Marco's back to indicate that he had done enough.

Shatterbug looked up at him, ready to punch him in defense before realizing what he was doing, and broke out of his apparent trance.

"I— I'm sorry, that was— I shouldn't be doing that."

"I agree. That was reckless and frightening. But it did what it needed to; this 'Disaster Pact' is rendered harmless." Null said, with no hint of judgment; good or bad.

"So what do they have to do with me?" Marco asked with eager curiosity.

"Unclear. Who ordered you to destroy the world?" Null looked down at Reactor, who seemed unharmed, though still resigned.

"No one. We were brought back to life by nature itself, and we had these powers. We took that as a hint." she responded. Reactor seemed to believe what she was claiming.

"Ah. How... disappointing. It would seem there are no answers here, either."

"Just more questions." Marco offered.

"Indeed. Though, these questions are not of my concern. These three are no longer problematic. It is the source of their power that is. Surely, whatever caused their transformation is also responsible for mine. But they remember no more than I; certainly, nothing any more helpful than what I already have."

"You're too caught up in your quest, Null. We saved the world, just now. That's something to celebrate!"

"You think these three were going to destroy the world? My defenses were hastily constructed; they were not very sturdy or powerful, and my ability largely filled in with regards to the specifics of their structure where I didn't need to. Your world would have handled them with ease—they are tiny."

The grey-clothed man's sudden disregard for the significance of others caught Marco off guard, questioning the morality of the man he considered, for a moment, a friend. "No one is tiny, Null."

"No. Quite right. They are simply irrelevant, in the grand scheme of things. You and I, we are important, we are shapers of reality. They are... anarchists. They will be forgotten.

"Still, thank you for your assistance. It is clear to me that I will not find answers here. Perhaps I need to look somewhere more... influential to find understanding. You have my appreciation, Marco Nieve. I look forward to seeing what legacy you leave upon this world."

Marco blinked.

Null was gone, and Marco was left with the three members of the Disaster Pact, two still contained in their thin crystalline cages.

"Do not attack this city again. I can face you without Null just as well as with him. This world is protected from forces more terrifying and dark than you." With that, Shatterbug walked away, down the road in the direction of downtown New Jackson to return to Snow Dynamics Enterprises.

A good distance away, concealed by cars long abandoned on a street long empty, a dark, shapeless, writhing mass hovered menacingly, observing the situation. For once, it was silent, even to itself. It floated there, concerned with the events which had unfolded before it; events that it did not put into motion.

Issue 7

Aftershocks

The phone in the CEO's office rang loudly, prompting Marco to answer it quickly. Every time he remembered that he needed to make a point of fixing the volume on his landline, he would immediately forget to do so. It didn't help, of course, that most of the phone calls he got required his immediate response, and the rest were brief, forgettable interruptions from his paperwork.

"The helicopter is ready, Mister Nieve." the voice on the other end informed him.

"Oh wow, already? Good, thank you Brendan." replied the CEO, politely hanging up. He wasn't quite ready to leave yet, but Marco had taken to heart months ago that even when one is in charge, one is rarely in control. He saved his work and logged out of the company desktop, exiting his office.

He thanked his secretary again as he opened the door into the stairwell, beginning his ascent to the roof.

The New Jackson Public Service Company was so far playing hardball with regards to signing onto the OmniGrid program. Marco was hopeful that the Red Mountain Project Company would be more open to the idea. Being the second-largest energy supplier in the state, they would have more incentive to look into the initiative in order to get a leg up on the competition. In an effort to bring home Snow Dynamics Enterprises' commitment to an arrangement, Marco requested that their next meeting take place in person, rather than via telecom. The helicopter, therefore, served as a means to make an impressive entrance.

Marco stepped out onto the roof, which had conveniently been constructed with a helicopter pad, making testing of marconium-powered air vehicles not only more practical, but also more likely. It wasn't a particularly dangerous process; the technology existed for electric helicopters with limited battery supplies, and had for years. Snow Dynamics' engineers simply scaled up the frame and fitted their own kinetic batteries in place of the obsolete lithium-ion ones used in the proof-of-concept designs. They were hardier and, naturally, capable of indefinite flight.

This one, *Hero 4*, had been flown in from its garage at the large-scale prototyping facility in the outer edges of the suburbs. It didn't employ as many people as the manufacturing plant or even the corporate office, as it was merely a location for the company to experiment with technologies too large or too unstable for the cramped quarters of the downtown area. The helicopter wasn't so much ready—as Brendan had put it—as it was simply here. Of course, the distinction didn't really matter enough to correct.

The CEO walked across the helipad to his awaiting negotiations team, waving cheerily to the pilot.

Before he had even made it halfway across the roof, a figure seemed to fall out of the sky, crashing right in front of Marco and causing him to fall back in surprise.

As the dust settled, he looked up at the source of the disturbance. Before him stood a person in a gold or brass-plated suit, not much more reinforced than the Shatterbug armor. There was a distinctive hexagonal pattern etched into the material, almost giving the appearance of scales. The undersuit, which also seemed to borrow heavily from that of Marco's own, was a black material that he suspected was just as durable as Shatterbug's. Rather than a domed glass visor, however, the person before him wore a menacing helmet. Around the jaw, it looked like a dark iron or gunmetal grey; there was no place through which a mouth could be seen, and a cone extended about an inch out from where the figure's nose would be. Above the grey portion, the mask extended upward with an unsaturated crimson material, easing to a point at the top of the helmet. Two rectangular holes for eyes were present, but they glowed a sickly yellow-green, straight through Marco.

"Visor on." he said without hesitation. He had been working on his response times when confronted with a surprise attack for just this occasion. The Shatterbug suit heard him, and responded to the command appropriately; the strange necklace unfolded itself up behind his head, and having established a frame, released the four glass pieces which merged together to form his bubble-like visor. "Gary, get the team in there now. Shattershock!"

Marco stood up quickly in the present. He saw his duplicates were doing the same, though the one in the past was all alone on the roof. His opponent simply stared back at him intently, fists clenched at the sides in preparation.

In his own time, Shatterbug charged for the attacker, pulling back his arm. He realized this was incredibly telegraphed, of course, but at the force it would be impacting with, there was no way to counter his blow. He extended his arm forward into his opponent and shouted "Reconstitute!"

The figure before him reached out his fist as well to meet him, in a futile attempt to counter the hero's attack. At the moment their knuckles connected, all three versions of Shatterbug folded into the present, sending the force of time into their extending arm.

The two fists united, but Marco's opponent didn't react. They barely even flinched. He had timed it perfectly, as always, yet it was as though it had no effect.

"Surprised, Shatterbug?" the figure spoke. Marco could now unmistakably tell that the voice belonged to a man, although it was labored a bit by the heavy mask.

"How are you—?" was all he was able to stutter.

The gold-suited man pulled his arm back quickly, then turned on his heel to gather momentum so as to kick Shatterbug in the stomach, sending him back to the ground. "Marconium suit." he replied.

"That's not possible; all marconium research is done at Snow Dynamics."

"Perhaps you are not as infallible as you have come to believe. Then again, you never were afraid to admit your own shortcomings." the villain sneered.

"You don't know anything about me, *pendejo*." he replied. Marco didn't much like to swear, but situations like this called for it. And it didn't count in an unfamiliar language, right?

"Ah, the fire is new. You've grown up quite a bit. From boy to bastard." continued the masked man. "I know you more than you realize, Mister Nieve. I am the Hellbent. Hellbent on taking you down."

Marco couldn't help but let out a loud, exasperated, confused, "WHY?! What could I possibly have done to you?"

"Good to see you still haven't lost your naiveté. Of course, I don't expect you to know what you've done to me; that's the point of the mask. I don't expect you to know what you've done at all. This isn't a lesson, this is revenge."

Marco muttered under his breath. "Gary, what have you got for me?"

"Sorry sir," began a new voice within the helmet. "We didn't know you were going on a mission, we're still gathering everyone."

"Neither did I!" he shouted into the suit. "Give me what you've got; you don't all need to be there!"

"Do not." the Hellbent said, as if the voices on the other end of Marco's conversation could hear him. "This is between you and me, Nieve."

Marco had yet to actually stand up, so the Hellbent took the opportunity to try to smash his armored foot into him. He was only able to shout "Shattershock!" just before the impact.

The villain hit the present Shatterbug hard. Although the suit did protect him from serious injury, it was still a painful experience.

His future version called out "Reconstitute!" as his punch five minutes ahead connected with the Hellbent, and the sore Marco in the present was pulled into the future to aid in his attack.

Again, however, the gold-colored armor of the Hellbent was able to withstand the blow with only a reactionary shake. He shattershocked again.

The Hellbent attempted to swing his marconium-powered leg into a roundhouse kick, but the Marco in the present reconstituted again, attempting to land another time-bending attack on his opponent. Once more though, the masked man's suit protected him completely.

"I knew this suit would be able to withstand your punches, Nieve," the stranger's obstructed voice began as he tried to swing into Marco with a solid right hook. "But I didn't expect that you would be this hard to hit!"

Shatterbug reconstituted into the future, again failing to bring any harm to the Hellbent.

"Are you ready to give up, then?" Marco dared of the villain.

"Yes." he replied, lowering his fists. "For the moment."

The Hellbent jumped up. It was an impressive height for a human—no doubt aided by the marconium-powered armor—but it was far from being superhuman. It was enough, though, to allow for a strange hovering platform to quickly fly under its owner just before he reached the peak of his ascent. He looked down at the hero from his new perch.

"You'll taste my vengeance quite soon, Shatterbug. Don't get too comfortable." With that, the Hellbent flew away on his peculiar hoverpad, out of sight. The helicopter was unharmed, but no longer running.

Again, Marco attempted to reach out through his suit's communication system. "Gary— *que demonios*! What happened there?"

"Sorry, sir, we're not sure. We just... didn't *want* to give you any advice." the voice responded.

"What is that supposed to— never mind. I'm coming down there." Marco was infuriated. Didn't want to give any advice? That was their entire job description!

He told the pilot to return the chopper to its garage, and asked that the negotiations team postpone their meeting with Red Mountain Project on account of an attempt on his life. He descended with them back into the building. Marco purposefully didn't bother to pick up his discarded business suit, and yet he couldn't help but think that he was forgetting to do something.

Marco stormed into the room full of the dozen or so Snow Dynamics employees, entitled the Operators. After some tinkering with the Shatterbug outfit, the company's researchers found that a small module could be appended to the back of the suit, allowing not only for communication with the wearer, but also for the transmitting of video data from the visor's included camera. A new department was formalized, therefore, with the task of working together with Shatterbug while on missions, providing additional insight by seeing what Marco sees, researching as necessary and relaying strategies for handling unique situations.

Gary Thornton was the director of the Operators Department, and was responsible for gathering the team together in emergency situations. He was also the one who spoke on behalf of the department during a mission. In this case, however, that meant owning up to what had just transpired on the roof.

"Marco, I know you're upset, but please listen to me." the man began, his Yorkshire accent clear, but not distracting. "We can't really explain what happened there or why. I meant no ill-intent when I said... what I said—"

"You said you didn't want to help me. How is that not ill-intended?" Marco was trying, but struggling, to maintain his professionalism.

"Again, I know how it sounds. I don't have an explanation for you, but I do have the beginnings of some findings."

"Show me." ordered Mr. Nieve.

Gary pulled up the windows from his screen onto the large wall monitor at the front of the Operator room. Images that were pulled from the fight on the roof had been ripped from the video files, showing the menacing figure of the Hellbent. He walked down the aisle of desks to the big screen.

"Now obviously, as he told you, his suit is powered by marconium, like yours. In fact much of the design is clearly borrowed from the Shatterbug armor, though obviously it has noticeably more substance. However, having personally been watching, and from the little data we've extrapolated so far, it appears he wasn't using any sort of time distortion, which is good news."

Marco was calming down some, but didn't let it show. "How was he deflecting my attacks? I couldn't scratch him at all, it was like I wasn't even reconstituting."

"Without having the suit in front of me I couldn't begin to accurately determine how he's doing it. If I had to guess from the footage, I would say the marconium power is being used to vibrate the plates, and perhaps even the undersuit, to such a degree and in such a manner that they naturally counter the forces your suit creates. If that is correct, that would also explain why your punches still cause a slight reaction; it's not hurting him on account of the armor, but it's interrupting the vibrations of the plate you're making contact with, which would be discomforting when the entire rest of one's body is shaking. But again, that's only a hypothesis for the moment."

Marco was impressed. "Do you have any ideas on countering it, when he does make another appearance?"

"Just one. And it isn't a guarantee, as it's based on that observation. The Uniform Program has recently made some progress that I believe may be able to hold its own against the Hellbent." Gary began to walk out, motioning for his employer to follow him.

The two men walked down the hall to the elevator. Gary was leading the way, although Marco did know where they were going. They rode down from the twelfth floor to the eighth, exiting and making an immediate right into one of the workshops.

"Oh, Mister Nieve!" one of the scientists exclaimed. Marco did make a point of visiting the various programs regularly, but generally called ahead to inform the staff. "And Director Thornton?"

"I understand you've made some progress?" asked the CEO, still in his superhero outfit.

"Er, well, still no."

"Not that part," Gary interjected before Marco could respond. "The tangential project."

"Oh, yes, of course!"

"But fill me in on where we are on the main program, as well." Marco asked politely. The Uniform Program was one of the most important in the company, if only to Marco. It was tasked with examining the Shatterbug armor in an attempt to determine how it performs the time travel mechanics. Of course, they couldn't have constant unchecked access to the suit, so they spent several days drawing up blueprints for it—under supervision. Largely, their experiments were done by trying to recreate the suit. If that wasn't producing results, Mister Nieve needed to be aware.

"Well," began the scientist. "We've been able to successfully construct a perfect replica of the Shatterbug outfit, including synthesizing the unusual material of the undersuit. It lines up with the blueprints exactly. We're still not certain how the various modules allow for time travel, but that's beside the point.

"Once the new suit was built, we tried simply putting a marconium battery in it; modules beneath the plates all activated, but the warmth you described to have come from the core didn't occur, and of course, nothing happened once the cycle completed."

"So then that's why you asked to see the core again?" Marco thought aloud.

"Correct; we thought that perhaps there was something about the original core in particular that allowed for the process. We built a new battery with a glass casing, like yours, for an apparently superficial additional sample to be contained in. It was laser cut to the exact measurements and specifications as the original sample—for all intents and purposes, it was a perfect duplicate down to the atomic level. In the tests following, the warmth was present, but still yielded no results."

Marco was disappointed with this. It did provide some new hypotheses for the source of the ability, but produced no actual conclusions. Again. "Thank you. Moving on; what else have you accomplished?"

"Since we couldn't get a new Shatterbug suit to work, we started trying to find new ways to use marconium power for wearable technologies like it. This suit in particular looks to be very promising." The scientist walked over to the wall, where a number of containment tanks had been erected. All but two were empty; Marco and Gary were led to the first one.

Pressing a button, their guide opened the door to reveal an orange suit. It had purple plates across its body, though in more places than the Shatterbug armor, most notably on its forearms and the backs of its hands. The visor was the same as Marco's, though the top of the frame dipped down a bit further to form a 'V' out of the reflective glass bubble, which was also tinted slightly orange. Some purple trim was used where the circuits connected the modules together, and the hands appeared to have grips on the insides. The marconium battery was visible, but was a simple metal cylinder, rather than the showy glass case of its muse. The metal around the window looked like it might turn, like a dial.

"We call this the Shockdrop suit." the Uniform Program scientist continued. "When the hands are clapped together, or at higher settings, when they come into contact with anything, it produces shockwaves with magnitude relative to the force at which contact was made. The direction and range of these waves can be controlled based on how you create the impact. The plates provide an inherent defense for the user from their own power, and we've ensured that the shockwaves' frequencies are always inhibited such that they can't level buildings or rip people apart. The Shatterbug suit should also be protected from the effects of this one. With practice, you could even land from a great height in such a way that the shockwaves allow you to walk away unharmed."

The scientist finished his presentation, leaving Marco impressed and Gary unscathed. However, the CEO's brow was furrowed with concern before long.

"I don't know that I have the time to learn a new suit. And besides, the Shatterbug armor is important. Its powers go beyond just punching, I need to have the time jumping at my disposal. Is there a way to incorporate these mechanics into my own outfit?" he expressed gently.

"I don't believe there would be, no." the scientist answered.

"Perhaps we could find a volunteer to pilot the Shockdrop outfit alongside Shatterbug?" Thornton offered.

Marco liked that idea. A sidekick. A partner. That would be ideal, not only for handling this Hellbent person, but also to help fight this darkness, whatever and wherever it was. But who? As much as he did trust his employees, he felt that the Shockdrop identity should fall to someone outside the company. Someone with experience and physicality, who could use Snow Dynamics' resources with him without taking away from their own responsibilities.

For some reason, only one person came to mind. It wouldn't have been anyone else's first choice, but Marco felt that it would work out the best. Not to mention, he needed to think quickly and be prepared for the Hellbent's next move.

"Shattershock!" Marco bellowed, not out of anger or exasperation, but to make clear his intentions to his opponent.

The man across the room, in all three times, charged straight for Shatterbug. Once he was close, he leapt into the air, clearly planning to come down at Marco with a crushing jab of his fist. Marco reconstituted as his own fist lined up with the other man's, but as his three selves returned to the present, his opponent seemed to change his attack, slapping his own fist and creating a shockwave to push Marco back and out of the way, avoiding the impact of the reconstitution.

He hadn't been knocked down, but was thrown slightly off balance from sliding across the concrete floor. He looked up after having steadied himself. Shockdrop's visor was mirrored, like his own, but from his body language, Marco could tell that Miguel was grinning like a fool inside. He'd managed to trick Shatterbug, land a blow—if indirectly—and dodge his counterattack. A first for each.

Miguel Jimenez had spent the last two days training extensively with the Shockdrop armor. Marco was pleasantly surprised the Hellbent had granted them this much time, but he couldn't complain.

He wasn't surprised, yesterday, when Miguel was more than eager to join his old roommate from freshman year in becoming a superhero. He had gotten into New Jackson State University on a football scholarship, and though he was an above-average student, he was still a jock through-and-through. Perfectly built for fighting crime, and perfectly minded for it, too. Since it was summer, Marco wasn't stealing him away from any classes. When the time came for Miguel to choose, Marco was sure they would find a place for him in the company. He hadn't dropped out yet, of course; that would be extreme.

The day prior had been spent having Miguel learn to use the suit in a general sense. The engineers, along with Marco, showed him how to control the intensity level and manipulate the direction of the shockwaves. Most of the day consisted of various obstacles or puzzles, allowing Miguel to experiment with different ways of using the Shockdrop armor's power, and doing so consistently.

Today, so far, was being used to spar. Miguel was confident in his understanding of the suit, and so the next step was using it effectively against opponents; against the Hellbent. Of course, the Shatterbug suit had defenses from the shockwaves in the same way Shockdrop was protected from them himself. The important part was ensuring he knew how to use his powers in a fight, as it was assumed he would have an advantage against the Hellbent's gold-plated armor.

"Good work, Miguel!" Marco applauded. "Visor off."

"Visor off." Shockdrop repeated, allowing his own helmet to close down into a similar orange neck brace. "That was awesome!"

"It was, but that was only once. I'm still up by three; and you still have a lot to improve on. The Hellbent is at a tactical advantage even to me, despite my privilege of seeing multiple times. Neither of us is ready for him yet, and we have no idea when he's going to strike." Marco was trying to be friendly, but it was important to be firm in this reminder.

"Oh *relajate*, I got it Marco. We'll be ready; it'll all be cool. ¡*No se preocupe*!"

"Alright, alright. Again." he instructed, returning to his side of the room. "Visor on."

"Visor on!" Miguel exclaimed excitedly.

The two heroes charged at each other with fists pulled back, prepared to meet. Shockdrop stopped short, instead clapping his hands together with violent force, creating a massive vertical shockwave, hurtling towards Shatterbug.

"Shattershock!" Marco shouted.

"Reconstitute!" called out the Marco in the future. All three Marcos again united, five minutes after the attack.

Shockdrop launched another, horizontal this time. Marco didn't get a chance to dodge it, though.

A crashing sound came from overhead, and a gold-plated capsule descended into the room of the large-scale Snow Dynamics facility through the resulting hole, following the light debris from the ceiling. It opened up like an egg, swallowing Shatterbug before either he or Shockdrop could react, then carried him away with its familiar helicopter rotor design. By the time the last shockwave reached, Marco was gone and his abductor was well out of the way.

It was dark inside the pod. Marco thought about shattershocking out, but was concerned that doing so would end up dropping him out of the sky with no support, as would reconstituting immediately in the present. So he submitted to his captor, which carried him to some unknown destination for several minutes. He maintained contact with his Operators, but they had limited data with which to track him while he was in the egg-shaped box. If there were a window, it would be another story.

This was almost certainly the Hellbent's doing. The shell of his flying prison was gold-colored exactly like the villain's suit, and Marco thought he recalled the same hexagonal pattern as well, though he didn't get a great look at it.

Finally, after what seemed like ages, the whirring of the machine slowed, and Marco no longer felt the rocking of his capsule. The bottom opened, coughing the hero out as the whole thing ascended, forcing him to his feet, then hovered away.

Shatterbug looked around him to get a sense of where he was—to give the Operators a sense of where he was.

114

The space he stood in now was somewhat expansive; not nearly as much so as where he had been taken from, but larger than an ordinary room. It was mostly a quartz-white with gold or yellow trimming all around. Various aeronautical systems were in some parts of the room: altimeters, barometers, and several other measurement devices that Marco was unfamiliar with—or more accurately, that were not labeled. It seemed to be laid out more like an arena than a bridge, but at the head of the space, in front of a large, cyclopean window, was indeed a pilot's station. As well as the Hellbent.

"Keep your eyes on the window!" Marco heard Mister Thornton say through the suit's communication system. "We're working on determining your location as quickly as we can."

Marco stared intently at his opponent, not that he could tell through the mirrored visor. "What are you doing, Hellbent?"

"Always asking questions, never trying to solve things for yourself. Typical, and pitiful. You are not fit to rule Snow Dynamics." spat the masked man.

"I don't rule it. We're a company, and we're doing good work—"

"You are squandering resources, wasting time! You are a hero, you are meant to be saving the world! But all you've done is contribute to society's failure."

"You're wrong!" Marco charged at the Hellbent in anger. "Shattershock!"

Marco noticed in the past and future that he was standing in different positions in the room than in the present. Whatever he was in was moving—slowly, thankfully, so he was still safe inside. He would need to take that into account.

Continuing as he thought this, Shatterbug began his lunge towards his opponent. But in all three times, the Hellbent crouched down, turning on one heel with expert acrobatics skills, tripping the time-strewn hero over his extended leg.

As all three began to fall, the Marco in the future was able to catch himself more easily, and seized the opportunity. "Reconstitute!" he shouted, using his feint of a fall to kick the Hellbent at the moment of time's reunion.

The force was still not enough to do anything through the gold suit, though, and without the follow-through, Shatterbug fell to the ground anyway.

"Perseverance has gotten you so far, Nieve. Now, though, your only real talent will fail you." Although he couldn't see the Hellbent's face, Marco was positive he was smirking with cruel mirth beneath the iron mask.

Marco heard a crash for the second time today, but this time, its origin was the floor. The airship had been breached from below!

Marco turned around to see what happened. The projectile had shot through the bottom of the ship, arcing inside the room and landing between the hole and the two combatants. Standing there, with a triumphant and proud pose, was Miguel Jimenez in the Shockdrop armor.

"There are two of you now?" the Hellbent groaned with annoyance. "Your time powers are useless to me. I built this suit myself; no number of Shatterbugs can harm me."

"I'm not Shatterbug." Miguel said, clearly excited and having practiced for the perfect way to introduce himself. He slammed his hands together, creating a horizontal shockwave

116

which passed over Marco's head, but slammed into the Hellbent, pushing him back and into the steering systems, breaking them under the weight of his suit. "The name's Shockdrop!"

"No..." grumbled the Hellbent, getting back to his feet. He held out his open hand to Shockdrop across the room. "This I cannot allow."

Shockdrop froze, as if under a spell. He walked slowly and silently to the hole in the floor, impressively calmly, despite the blaring of the alarms and the force of the airship falling slowly to the Earth.

"Miguel, what are you doing?!" Marco shouted to his friend, rising to his feet.

"What he wants to do." the Hellbent replied for him. "Which conveniently, is exactly what I want him to do."

"What? What is that supposed to—?"

"The will of humanity is mine to bend as I please. Anyone— everyone on Earth is a tool, ready and willing to serve my agenda. Not that they would recognize it as anyone's choice but their own. 'Miguel' has no idea that I am ordering for him to do this; he is more than happy to comply with his own mind."

"You're insane! You're a monster!"

"And you are a fool, Marco Nieve!" the man shouted, his sickly eyes glowing beneath his mask as they glared through Shatterbug's visor. "I want to make you feel my vengeance; this is why I have not manipulated your will. But I am not above commanding the minds of everyone around you to hurt you!"

A range of emotions Marco had never felt collectively before washed over him. Guilt, anger, hate, fear, and so many more swelled in his mind as Shockdrop drew closer to the hole in the crashing skyship. Null had been an ally, but Miguel was a friend. He would not lose him.

"Shattershock!" Marco let out with all of his heart. His suit reacted as if it understood his anger, violently splitting him into three copies across time. However, as the airship the present Shatterbug was in was currently falling, both the past and future Marcos were left in the sky, and began to plummet to the ground; one above the ship and one below.

Both the Shatterbug in the past and in the future shouted in tandem. "Shattershock!"

Each of the suits at either end of the rip in time began to whir to life. Although they were falling, both Marcos could feel the plates across their outfits vibrate, and the marconium cores in front of their chests warmed, creating an additional Shatterbug twenty-five minutes further in the past and future, for a total of five Marco Nieves, scattered across an hour of time.

Both of the new Shatterbugs were also falling through the sky, but that didn't matter. In the present, Marco extended his fist towards the Hellbent, whose full attention was on the enslaved Shockdrop. As his fist collided with the side of the villain's mask, he shouted with fury: "Reconstitute!"

All five Shatterbugs folded back into the present, taking with them the full force of sixty minutes of time being united into one moment once more, slightly cracking the mask and, more importantly, sending the Hellbent flying. His ragdoll of a body slammed into and broke one of the side windows, and he too began to fall outside the relative safety of his airship.

With the Hellbent's attention diverted, Shockdrop's mind was now free, and he backed away from the hole he was merely steps away from.

"Miguel, the ship is falling!" Marco shouted over the alarms.

"What do we do?!" Miguel responded with equal volume.

"Jump!" Gary shouted to the two heroes through the suits. "Shockdrop can protect you! Land on your fists at the highest setting, the shockwaves will cushion you!"

Shatterbug and Shockdrop both looked at the other. They grabbed each other's hands, and dove into the hole of the falling skyship.

With some effort, they were able to angle their bodies vertically and upside down. The blood rushed from their heads, but fortunately they were close enough to the ground now that they didn't black out before Miguel was able to extend his fists outward—one still intertwined with Marco's—and smash into the Earth with maximum force.

They had landed safely, but as they got up, Marco was the first to realize. "There's still a massive blimp falling down right on top of us!"

"Go to the future! See where the closest spot is to stand where we won't get hit!" Miguel yelled. A brilliant idea. Why hadn't Marco thought of it?

"Shattershock!" he shouted. In the future, Marco could see that the surface damage was extensive and widespread, though thankfully in a rather open area, as of yet undeveloped by the nearby neighborhoods. He spotted a space twenty feet from them, where the crash would create a small pocket, covered by but protected from a sheet of fallen metal. The present Marco guided himself and Shockdrop to that position before reconstituting, just in time for the Hellbent's ship to come crashing down over them.

As Marco predicted, the two heroes were protected by a piece of the airship which came down over them, rather than onto them.

"*Santo cielo*, that was insane, man!" Miguel shouted ecstatically. "Did you see how I blew through that ship? And wow, did I stick that landing or what?"

"That was pretty cool, dude." Marco said, trailing off slightly.

He noticed in the distance a shape that could only be the Hellbent, escaping on his hoverpad. He couldn't tell from this distance, of course, but Marco was sure that the villain probably felt decidedly defeated.

"Alright, let's get out of this mess and back home. Think you can handle some wreckage?" he said to his partner, smiling through the mirrored visor.

With a decisive punch in the air, Shockdrop made clear his enthusiasm and took the lead, shoving aside the rubble to create a passage for the armored pair.

The dark, malignant being watched the two heroes proudly walk away, ignorant of the true reason they were spared a fiery demise. How could they have noticed, though, that *it* was holding up the refuse which shielded them from the rest of the impact? They would not even think to look.

"My gratitudes for your oblivious collaboration, Doctor Strauss." the creature mused to itself, elongating each word as always. It never grew tired of hearing itself speak in this guttural tongue. "It will bring you solace to know that your findings will not go unappreciated. Of course, they will do *you* little good."

It shrieked with delight at the perfection with which its scheme had unfolded over these several months. It had enjoyed gently pulling the strings of its heedless marionettes, but the games were nearing their completion.

Issue 8
Cosmic Intervention

Miguel slammed his fists together, generating a shockwave which hurtled down the street.

Marco, a few hundred feet away, excitedly commanded to his suit: "Shattershock!"

Two copies of Shatterbug appeared in the past and future, however Shockdrop had been practicing, and in those times created two more horizontal shockwaves in the direction of his opponent. No one else was on the abandoned street. It was hero versus hero.

With no way to jump through time to avoid Miguel's attacks, the Marco in the future gave the order once more. "Shattershock!"

Another Shatterbug, twenty-five minutes ahead, saw an opening in Shockdrop's attention, and reconstituted to dodge all three shockwaves quickly approaching his duplicates in the past.

With the unveiling of the new marconium suit, and the defeat of the Hellbent three weeks ago, Marco Nieve, Miguel Jimenez, and Snow Dynamics Enterprises were rising to national fame. They knew they would never be able to put a stop to all crime, and they had no intention of taking away from the respect of law enforcement agencies. But, the public wanted something flashy and unique; individuals of merit and impress to look up to. Shatterbug and Shockdrop were those heroes. That is, when they weren't trying to really save the world.

Snow Dynamics had reached an agreement with the Red Mountain Project, which was nearing completion of the transition to supplying marconium energy to its consumers in the state of New Jackson. Once the successes began to speak for themselves, Marco hoped that other energy corporations like the New Jackson Public Service Company, or even others across the country, would be calling to sign on to the OmniGrid Program.

Today was not about solving the world's energy crisis, though. In the interest of creating conversation for the company and for the heroic intentions of all its employees, Marco had worked with the city—with the support of Mayor Henry Frederick, who took over from his former position of Deputy Mayor—to empty this street for him and Miguel to perform a sort of exhibition match. As the Shockdrop suit was harmless to buildings, Snow Dynamics had invited hundreds of people from the city to attend, free of charge, to watch the spectacle of the two superheroes from the safety of the various local shops and eateries along Central Avenue.

"Shattershock!" Marco shouted, with all three versions going three separate directions in an attempt to reach his opponent, who was relying solely on long-range attacks. In this capacity, he continued his battering of wave after wave of marconium-excited pressure, trying to hit the Shatterbugs.

However his aim, Marco found, was much less extensive when his target was moving alongside him, rather than directly towards him. His past and future selves were following this line of attack, and so when the present Shatterbug would have been hit, he found himself pulled into the future by that copy's reconstitution.

Again, Marco shattershocked, this time having all three of his selves charge at Shockdrop indirectly. They encircled him, each preparing an attack on three different sides, in three different times. The past Marco had the best opening, and so he shouted, "Reconstitute!"

The three Shatterbugs folded together into one moment of time, the moment at which his fist would collide with Miguel's own, outstretched in anticipation. However, rather than create an impact of time, and therefore an enormous shockwave, both heroes were pushed back and away from each other. Blinded by a fantastic light, they fell to the ground in a daze.

Marco looked up, struggling to get to his feet at first. Between him and Miguel, where they had just been standing, hovered a blue man.

At first glance, that is. It looked like a man, and it looked blue. As his eyes refocused, Marco was able to get a better look at the figure. It floated there idly, as if the act of flight required no physical strain or mental focus. It had the silhouette of a man without clothes—though lacking any signs of gender outside of general build. Marco wasn't convinced it was a man, though. Largely, because it was not opaque.

The being appeared to be comprised of a blue or teal translucent light, with small specks of white light dancing unsupported within its frame. It had no other physical traits; no hair, clothes, or even surface features, with the exception of its face.

Its eyes, mouth, and nostrils were also made up of the white light which was contained within it, rather than the same blue hue of the rest of its body. There were no pupils or lips. Only the light.

"Marco Nieve." it spoke. Unlike Null's voice, which was indisputably plain and without feature, this being had a distinctive English accent. But even from just those two words, Marco could tell this was not true English; it was his own idea of it. What he imagined a superior being would sound like—what he expected Null to sound like.

"Who's asking?" Marco was still not on board with admitting his identity to strange beings that appeared out of nowhere, even if they were well informed and were likely without doubt of who he was and what he looked like.

"Relinquish the time machine." the being commanded.

"Don't think so. Shattershock!" he replied. Miguel, too, was not having any of this, and charged towards the energy-man from behind.

The silhouette of light turned in the air with ease, and as it was translucent, Marco could see it extend its arm and direct its palm to the oncoming attack. It didn't move beyond that, but when Shockdrop leapt up to punch the alien, a stream of shining blue light was released from its hand, firing Miguel into the street and back, leaving a wake of broken asphalt.

It turned back to face Marco.

"What are you?" he said in awe, and in fear of the being before him.

"I am Timegaze. I am the incarnation of the laws of time, and their protector."

125

"How... humble." Miguel coughed from behind it. It flashed its palms, presumably as a threat, prompting a response from Shockdrop. "Alright, alright; relax! *Dios mio...*"

"Time travel was never meant to be accessible to mortals in any universe," Timegaze continued. "Much less used so flippantly. Your intentions have been taken into account, and there will be no consequence if the time machine is relinquished now."

"If you know my intentions, you understand that I am being careful! I'm not creating paradoxes, I'm not changing any history!" Marco pleaded with the cosmic being.

"Your actions have been taken into account only to determine whether you were deserving of punishment. There is no excuse for the continued possession of time travel; it is dangerous to reality's stability, no matter the use, no matter how careful." It was clear the being was not giving up its mission. "Remove the armor before your judgment is adjusted."

Shatterbug charged towards Timegaze in the past, present, and future. It floated motionless where it was, not even moving its arm as it had with Miguel. The Shatterbug copy in the present reconstituted, and as he would have hit the floating light, shattershocked again.

Immediately, the Marco in the past took advantage of this opportunity to surprise Timegaze, giving the command to his suit just as his fist connected with the being's chest. "Reconstitute!"

But Timegaze wasn't surprised. It slapped the past Marco aside with ease, as though it was aware of the hero's plan the whole time.

"How did you do that...?" he muttered from the ground, confused.

"Got anything for us, Gary?" Miguel spoke into his own suit to request the Operator team's input.

"We have no idea. It looked like this Timegaze turned to where Marco was going to appear from the... future?" he replied. The Operators were helpful in researching and coming up with strategies, but their ability to interpret data about how time was affected by the Shatterbug armor was still limited to their own human comprehension.

"It knew I was going to time travel, and when?" Marco said in shock.

The being's eyes glowed brighter, releasing another stream of energy directly at Marco, forcing him back and into the wall of one of the stores lining the road.

Miguel got up now and, believing he had an advantage, crashed his fists together to create a vertical shockwave, expanding with unprecedented speed and power towards the alien of energy.

However, Shockdrop's attack passed over it harmlessly, as though it didn't even exist.

"Miguel, we picked up some distortion when your attack landed just then." Gary began to inform the hero. "Your attacks won't work on it, either; it's time jumping!"

Timegaze turned to face Shatterbug once again. "Relinquish the time machine."

"I can't do that!" Marco exclaimed.

In any other situation he may simply have not wanted to listen to a being claiming to be a god; but here, he truly could not obey. He was given the suit for a reason. Something major was coming, something that only he could stop. If anything, he should be asking Timegaze for help, not fighting it. It was clear, though, that the dazzling entity was uninterested in compromise.

"Mister Nieve, we've laid out a plan!" Marco heard Gary shout into his suit. "If what we've gathered about this Timegaze is correct, there may be a way to stop it! Try to lure it to the office building, we'll begin preparations here."

That worked for him. They were down the road quite a ways, but Marco could see the Snow Dynamics Enterprises headquarters a few blocks ahead of him, behind the cosmic being. "Did you get that, Miguel?" he said to his partner.

"Copy that, boss." Shockdrop replied, slamming his fists together again, launching another ripple of pressure at Timegaze. Although it didn't affect the entity, it turned to face its attacker anyway. It raised both its palms to release two bursts of energy at the hero, sending him flying back, closer to their destination.

Marco shattershocked, and all three versions attempted to move around Timegaze, to get on the same side of it as Miguel. It turned to face him in all three times, firing off another stream of light at him. The future Shatterbug was further ahead than the others, and so reconstituted together there, only to be launched sideways into the adjacent building. Again he split himself into three copies in time, each trying to move further down Central Avenue.

In the present, Timegaze once again sent forth an attack, directed toward the fleeing Shatterbug. Marco braced for impact, but was shoved aside, not far enough to hit the wall again, but out of the way of the brilliant attack. Shockdrop had created a wave to push his teammate out of the way.

The two heroes continued to run down the middle of the road, avoiding Timegaze's attacks while still attempting to hurt it when they could, if only to keep it interested and on their tail.

No matter how many Shatterbugs there were or when in time they existed, Timegaze was always right behind him. Marco tried to stay in the moments that Miguel was still nearby in. He had become skilled now at using his power to not only nudge Marco aside, but also himself, with some clever angling and reflecting of his shockwaves, to dodge the entity's light streams.

Finally, the three combatants reached the intersection on the corner of Snow Dynamics. Traffic had been blocked here, too, but only just recently. The company's employees had set up makeshift barriers at the three formerly-functional roads connecting to the barricaded portion of Central Avenue. The machine which had been placed in the middle of the crossroads was too large to safely allow cars to pass by.

Marco recognized the machine, but Mr. Thornton began to explain it through the suit's systems anyway. "The Event Horizon Simulator will create an incredibly small, incredibly dense portion of space; nowhere near powerful enough to become a black hole, but with enough of a gravitational field to slightly slow down time relative to the space outside its influence. Get Timegaze close and we'll turn it on, hopefully rendering its omnitemporality irrelevant."

"Come and get me, blue boy!" Shockdrop goaded, inciting another attack from Timegaze as they drew closer to the device.

Marco and Miguel reached the machine, and noting this, the Operators switched it on. The magnetic rings inside it began to spin and turn like a gyroscope, and various lights flashed and flickered all around it. The energy afforded it by ten marconium batteries allowed the machine to compress the air particles within the central chamber, taking in more and more from outside and crushing it down into a superdense pocket of benign elements.

At first glance, the two heroes were ignorant to its effects. But, as they looked at the cars outside the Simulator's invisible bubble, they could see that the people inside them and walking about seemed to be moving more quickly, like a tape being wound forward. Even the sounds of their honking horns were reduced to short, sped-up whines. Had Gary not just explained the effects to them, they might have thought the world around them was moving faster. In truth, they understood that they were moving much more slowly.

As was Timegaze. To Shatterbug and Shockdrop, the cosmic being was behaving as normal, which meant it was under the effects of the Event Horizon Simulator. Miguel clapped his hands together to let off a vertical shockwave in the direction of their opponent.

Like before, the entity did not budge. However this time, as the wave of pressure washed over it, Timegaze winced forward in discomfort. Its eyes glowed much more brightly now, as if in fear, and it flew quickly towards the heroes.

It grabbed hold of both of them by their necks; not choking them, but lifting them into the air. Its palms began to light up as it prepared another attack. Marco shattershocked, and this time, his version in the past was able to reconstitute with an uppercut into Timegaze's abdomen. Once again it reacted as though its power was useless, though Marco wouldn't exactly call it pain.

As Shockdrop was not being choked in the past, he too attempted to deliver a blow to the floating alien. Miguel used his shockwaves to propel himself into the air, getting himself to a height at which he could lay into Timegaze's face with a solid right hook.

The attack knocked Timegaze out of focus and off balance, as the ripple of space forced him to the ground with the rest of the world.

Now standing on its legs, its face lit up to fire another stream of energy at Marco.

"Shattershock!" he bellowed.

"Reconstitute!" shouted his future self, travelling five minutes ahead of the attack, where Shockdrop once again struck the being, sending it flailing wildly.

Although it wasn't what any of the spectators signed up for, Marco imagined that what was transpiring looked to be an impressive display of hand-to-hand combat, as Shatterbug and Shockdrop both subjected the weakened cosmic entity to an incessant pummeling. And yet through all of it, Marco still wasn't getting the impression that they were actually harming it.

"Enough!" it finally commanded, loudly but without emotion. It stretched its arms out, its hands and eyes shining spectacularly, but not firing attacks. The machine halted, and the two heroes stood motionless. Time had gone silent.

"I yield to you, Marco Nieve." Timegaze expressed with clear respect. "You faced me not with anger or greed, but with purpose and responsibility. I see the importance of your time machine."

The being's eyes and hands returned to their normal luminosity, and time once again turned as it was meant to. The machine remained off.

"I will allow you to keep it, so long as you continue to be reliable in your maintenance of the flow of time."

Marco bowed his head in reverence. "Thank you, Timegaze. I only want to do good for—"

"But know this:" it interrupted, coldly. "Should you fail to watch carefully the effects of your meddling with time, I will return, and I will not give you the opportunity to resist.

"You should also know that your foolishness is causing unseen forces to move in the background. If these forces threaten reality as a result of your pride, there will be consequences."

With that, Timegaze lifted itself from the ground once more, seemingly without effort. It rose into the sky, slowly at first, looking down at the two superheroes of Earth. As it rose higher, it accelerated faster, until it was out of sight completely.

"What's it talking about, unseen forces? Sounds like a ghost story to me." Miguel quipped.

"Miguel," Marco said solemnly. "Come inside. There's a story I need to tell you."

From the roof of Snow Dynamics Enterprises, the writhing mass of impossible darkness cautiously watched the scene below unfold. It had to stay small and hidden, even moreso than normal, while the cosmic being was nearby. Now, though, it was safe.

"If only you realized the futility of your warnings, angel of time." it growled mockingly, confident that its unwitting enemy was well and gone. "I am far more powerful than you can imagine. Still, I should redouble my efforts to remain... inconspicuous. But, there is so little left to conceal; your solace approaches."

For once, it allowed itself to express its elation much more vocally, such that were anyone paying attention, they might even be able to hear it. Of course, the insignificant mortals below would hardly be able to comprehend the resounding shrieks of its oppressive void, much less recognize it as their equivalent of laughter. And this knowing superiority over them only made it cry out more loudly and with more horrifying pleasure.

Issue 9
Genesis

It seemed to Marco that in the business world, whenever some great achievement was made, there would soon follow great strain and frustrations. Never due to the achievement itself, but rather due to resolving the budgeting, allocating, and negotiating that went into that achievement.

Such was the case when the Red Mountain Project completed the transition of their power grid, beginning their supply of energy generated by marconium power cells to their customers. It was sure to be a landmark in the history of the company and of the nation.

However, although marconium power requires little maintenance, and is cheap to operate once installed, it was still an expensive process. Because there is only so much marconium, and it is expensive to excavate from the mining operation in the Arctic Circle, the element tended to be financially volatile. Up to now, Snow Dynamics had not needed to be concerned about expenses, as the government contracts kept funding effectively constant. But while this transaction did not lose them money, they did lose out on profits by selling away some of the precious element at cost. This was all for the good of the world, of course, but it meant that other parts of the budget needed to be looked at to ensure as much of the company could remain functional as possible.

It was therefore Marco's job to work with his executive team in finding ways to cut spending, at least temporarily, without having to lay anyone off. To that end, they were devoting the week to seriously touring and examining every project and program in the building; going over resource purchases, scrutinizing archived marconium request forms, and inspecting timeframes to ensure all research was on schedule.

Today was the inspection of the military departments. To this day, Marco stood firm that marconium weapons research would never be undertaken. However, the government demanded that at least some funding had to be allocated to developing technologies that had general military applications, if not combat ones. Marconium powered non-lethal drones were the largest contract, and while there was no chance that any of these programs would be cut—at the risk of losing the associated funding—everything had to be looked at, if only to ensure there were no over-expenditures.

The first stop for the investigative team was the communications laboratories on the seventh floor. Here, new ideas for using marconium not only as a power source, but as a medium of information transmission were explored. This included not only audio and video, but also electricity. New microcircuit technologies like transistors, capacitors, and the like—anything that didn't yet exist was a goal for this department. Much of this would have flown over Marco's head, as he'd still been far too busy to be able to gather any more than a passing understanding of practical electrical systems; and these guys were working on highly advanced science. Fortunately for him, he and his executives were going to the military research division of the floor, which was much simpler, even if Marco didn't fully grasp the finer points.

"Good morning, Doctor Bedi." Ramirez greeted the lead scientist. "How is your day going?"

"I'm not sure yet. I suppose part of that will depend on what you decide about our work." Ryan Bedi replied cheerily. He had been hired shortly after the move to the current Snow Dynamics offices. He likely would have simply been a project technician, had Marco's first choice for the lead not requested to be transferred to a different department. He was a happy man with bright eyes, and was fiercely task-oriented.

"Well then let's begin, Doctor." Marco invited. "Please explain to us what your work consists of."

Naturally, Marco knew what he was doing here, but not all of the executive team were as interested in the day-to-day activities as he and Michelle. It also helped to get people talking before asking any harder questions. Of course, most knew that there was no risk of being laid off; they just didn't want to lose more of their budget than they had to.

Doctor Bedi turned about in excitement, beginning his rehearsed presentation. "This program focuses on fabricating new long-distance communication devices. We do have some radio-transmitters which are merely wired to run on marconium power, therefore allowing them to operate for longer periods of time over great lengths. However, most of the research is put into trying to develop new methods by which to transmit altogether.

"In this field, we have so far had the most promising results with this." The lead scientist switched on a large console in front of them. It looked to be a primitive computer, like what one might see in Cold War footage. It was large, grey, and had simple controls and a plain monitor, given the era. It began to beep slowly, apparently indicating it was working. "We don't have a name for it yet, as it's still under development. This will by no means be the final product; as we are working with effectively a new field of science, the technology needs to be very basic until we can expand upon it.

"At the moment, this device is capable of receiving telegraphic data. While it can pick up more complex information, Morse code is so far the most consistent. What is impressive about it is that it is completely wireless, and doesn't use any sort of satellite system beyond its own integrated receivers. We have been able to send communications to it from miles away, with obstructions being a non-issue to the quality of the reception. There is still much more work to go, but this promises to be a dramatic step forward in the field."

The machine continued to beep in rhythmic operation, and the various executives began to ask questions of the doctor.

"Is the program over-budget?"

"How much marconium have you used in the past three months?"

"Will this project be ready for production on schedule?"

It was their job to ask these questions, Marco understood. He should have been asking questions, too. But, for the moment, he was concerned more with the machine. More specifically, he was concerned with what the machine was doing.

The entire time they had been talking, since Doctor Bedi had turned it on, it had been beeping. Marco at first assumed, as he imagined the rest of his entourage had, that this was a standard of the machine; it meant it was functioning correctly. And yet, the longer Marco heard it, the more familiar it sounded.

He was no expert in Morse code, but years spent watching crime dramas on television had taught him one phrase. He never thought that knowledge would actually be useful, though.

"Doctor," Marco interrupted whoever was talking at the moment. "Are you performing any tests right now?"

Bedi looked a bit surprised by the disruption, but answered anyway. "Well I— uh, yes. As I said: we are testing frequently, in various circumstances to ensure—"

"No, I mean are you testing the machine right this moment?"

"No, I just turned it on to show you. Why?"

Marco nodded to it. The scientist hadn't been paying any attention to it, even now only just barely realizing something was wrong as he turned to the monitor, his eyes widening slowly.

"But, that's impossible... We've only ever picked up our own— no one and nothing else can transmit to this receiver." he declared with a tone that implied both surety and unconfidence.

The machine had been repeating the same three letters this entire time.

S-O-S.

The *Hero 2* helicopter flew high above the city of New Jackson, but its occupants were not interested enough to admire its beauty from this height. Their eyes remained solemnly transfixed on the floor, in silent contemplation.

The Operators were able to work with Doctor Bedi to find the source of the distress signal, but an explanation for how it was transmitting on marconium channels had not been found.

Marco had one theory. He could only tell Miguel, though, as he was the only other person who now knew the truth of how he had obtained the Shatterbug armor. If the doppelganger that gave him the suit was from the future, then it was possible that this cry for help also came from that same future. That made helping them his responsibility.

Director Thornton, of course, was concerned that it could be some sort of trap. The only other person outside of Snow Dynamics with access to marconium—inexplicable though it was—and the knowledge to use it was the Hellbent. To him, there was no other explanation.

Either way, they had no visual contact with the location of the signal; it was at the very edge of the city, just past where the suburbs became the desert. A decision had to be made.

Thus, Shatterbug and Shockdrop boarded the Snow Dynamics Enterprises helicopter, and flew out to investigate, if only from a distance.

The chopper touched down in the middle of the empty street. It was a surreal sight; before them, the two heroes could see the expanse of desert, stretching out for miles. There were towns out there, behind the Ghost Story Mountains, but for as far as they could see, it was unpopulated.

Even behind them was barely the greater New Jackson area. There was a small town a few hundred yards away, and some new developments were being built in the area, but even their construction hadn't reached this far out yet. Marco couldn't see the downtown skyline at all from here, despite the relatively flat expanse to the east.

Although Marco did admire the beauty of the desert, it was not why they were here. Before them, just a few dozen feet to the west, was a gaping hole in the world.

The interior of the hole was filled with a sort of rippling effect. It shone gold and purple and silver, like an otherworldly pond glistening in the sun—though it stood vertical, suspended above the ground. The hole's frame was made up of a fractal-like assemblage of swirling wisps, acting independently of the wind. They behaved as though they were holding the hole open, but they were so perfectly black that Marco was sure they could only be a feature of the pool.

Thornton spoke up again, now having established visual contact with the destination from Shatterbug and Shockdrop's visors. "The signal is definitely originating from that point."

"It looks like a portal." Miguel said admiringly.

"It's not; portals can't exist." Gary corrected. "Can you two please move around it? Try and look at it from all angles, something must be producing this effect as well as the signal."

The heroes did as instructed. They strafed about the abnormality opposite each other, moving around the sides and to the back from where they had begun.

Through all of this, the hole did not move. More accurately, it did not change the perspective that Marco and Miguel observed it at no matter where in space they were looking upon it from. It was always facing them, rippling and swirling ominously.

"That's not possible. It's like a convex-face illusion, but it goes all the way around... There's no source!" Gary was enthused and alarmed.

"Still looks like a portal to me."

"I'm going to touch it." Marco declared.

"It— no, no, don't do that!" Gary yelled into the suits.

"Why not? It's clearly a portal, which means the signal is coming through there. If someone needs help, I need to help them."

"We have no idea if it is a portal! And if it is, there's no way of knowing if the other side is safe, if you'll be able to return, or if we'll even be able to reach you!"

Marco tried to justify himself in his mind. If the signal was broadcasting Morse code to marconium receivers at Snow Dynamics, then it was using a marconium device to do it; which meant something intelligent was on the other side. Given the curiousness of the situation and its relation to the Shatterbug outfit, it was likely someone from the future. Because the signal was travelling through the portal, if he could get through, it could be concluded he could get back. The same would apply for communication across it.

"I'm doing it."

"Please, Mister Nieve, I implore you to return to headquarters and let us work together to form a safer strategy!" Director Thornton begged.

"I'm leaning with Gary on this one, *hermano.*" Miguel added.

But Shatterbug wasn't listening. Any way he turned it— whether it was someone who needed help, a trap set by the

Hellbent, or something else entirely—this was his responsibility. Whatever was on the other side of that hole knew it was contacting Marco, and only Marco.

He brought his hand to the surface of the rippling pool, and pushed in gently. It didn't feel like anything, but it looked like it should have. The surface of the portal fell inward slightly as he pressed against it, before seeming to break like a membrane, accepting him. There was no force pulling him, and the continued undulation of the hole didn't affect his body in any way.

He allowed more of his arm to pass through. Then, believing it to be safe, he walked into it completely, being sure to lift his legs over the twisting tails of the edges.

If Marco had marveled at the expanse of desert, he was blown away by the visage of where he now stood.

He looked in wonder at the cathedral which now housed him. The entirety of the structure was like a polished stony gold, carved and fashioned into a rotunda, almost resembling the Roman Pantheon. However, the space between the pillars was just that: space. There were no walls; they were like windows, looking out into nothingness.

The center of the room was dominated by some sort of art installation. It looked like art, anyway, as Marco had no comprehension of it. Twelve circular steps, each higher than the last, held the centerpiece in the air like a tiered cake. Atop them floated a sphere of some kind. It glittered in the same off-gold color as the rest of the room.

However, all of this admiration took place in merely a few fractions of a second; Marco realized immediately that he was not alone in the structure.

A penetrating mass of darkness hovered and writhed all around the room, surrounding both Marco and the raised sphere's platform. It was enormous, and seemed to be in every corner of the space in at least some capacity. Beyond its astounding, unsettling blackness, it had no features at all. Its tentacles wriggled and snaked all about, out of either excitement or boredom—or perhaps both. It looked to be holding several purple things, scattered about its winding, amorphous shape. They appeared to be what Marco imagined computer ghosts might look like: only the outline of their body was visible, and it was incomplete, constantly in motion like corrupted data. They didn't move from within the grasp of their bearer.

Marco turned around. In the moment, he wasn't sure whether it was to greet Shockdrop in the hopes he had followed, or to escape. But, as he did so, the portal closed. The winding tendrils which had indeed held it open retracted, and returned to their main form: the congregation of darkness.

"Apologies, Marco Nieve." the mass spoke. Its voice was almost painful in its horrifying indefinity. It echoed itself, preceding itself with whispers and following itself with growls. It pierced his ears and shook his bones. It agitated his eyes and twisted his stomach. The immense void slurred itself, taking care in pronouncing each syllable. It hissed those noises which would be made with a tongue, and cracked those sounds which would be clicked with a throat, but Marco suspected it had neither. Its voice seemed to be resounding from everywhere, but also sourced from above him, high in the air, as though it was both looking all around at Marco, and down at him. "Your sidekick was not invited."

"Shattershock." Marco said, attempting to mask his undeniable fear with confidence. He had been preparing more than half a year for this confrontation. There had been several times when he wasn't sure if he was already facing his enigmatic

143

goal, or even whether the darkness existed at all. Now, as he stood in the unfamiliar pantheon, he was certain he was exactly where he needed to be, and he would be prepared.

"That will do you little good, here." the aggregation of black tentacles teased, slowly. "In fact, it would be more to your benefit to remain reconstituted."

"You know how my— never mind. Where have you taken me, darkness?"

"One step at a time, hero. Clearly, introductions are in order. I cannot allow you to call me by such offensive titles, can I?

"I...

"Am...

"Solace..." The creature growled with smug egotism, admiring its own name as it spoke it. Marco would have been amused, were the being that surrounded him not absolutely terrifying.

"And these creatures in my tendrils are the De'Raj: beings tasked with maintaining the cyclic nature of reality. This is their— what you would translate to—Genesis Shrine. This is where each iteration of the universe is born and burned, over and over again." The condescension in the monster's unearthly voice was clear. It was enjoying presenting Marco with all of this new information, like he was a child.

"And why have you brought me here?" He consciously posed his question with the tone of an order. He knew he had failed here before, and that only gave him more confidence. Or, at least, inspired him to appear more confident.

Solace did not immediately react. It slowly lifted the six or seven creatures higher into the air. They barely registered the motion, moving according to their captor's puppetry. Marco looked on with confusion.

Suddenly, in just a blink, the monster *contracted* its tentacles which constricted the lesser cosmic beings, while also jutting numerous spike-like tendrils from all around, *impaling* its prisoners every which way, all in just one moment. The creatures *shattered*, their incomplete forms practically falling apart, fluttering to the ground like ashes. Through all of this, the building was disturbingly silent, save for Marco's gasp of shock, and the quiet, grumbling pleasure of the brutal, psychopathic void.

Long purple cords, like spines, slinked out of Solace's now loosened grips, coiling onto the floor, motionless. The De'Raj had been slaughtered.

"*One step at a time*, my dear Shatterbug." Solace harshly screeched, fully in control of its pace and tone.

"What have you done?" was all Marco could bring himself to say. He was in shock. He was horrified. And he was scared. What had he gotten himself into? Was he sure he was ready for this?

"Fret not, Marco Nieve. Their position will soon be filled. Now then, on to why I have orchestrated your presence here. Of course, I had not planned on having to go to such lengths as this, but you have exhausted my options."

"O— options?" Marco struggled to regain his voice. But, the pieces started to put themselves together now, which helped him to feel in control, building his conviction. "Like Titan Black, you mean?"

Solace grumbled, apparently in acknowledgement of his observation. "Originally, Titan Black was meant to incapacitate you, so I could take what I needed without having to bring you here. In his failure, it was made evident that brute force alone would not suffice to earn me my prize."

"He tried to warn me about you. You transformed him into that thing; you killed him! And then you forced him to live in pain anyway! You heartless—"

"Then I thought, perhaps, I could convince you to sacrifice yourself for my goals, and so persuaded your sniveling Mayor Liu to orchestrate a hostage crisis."

"The hostage— you were what Liu was talking about! You've been pulling strings for months, manipulating everything!" Marco wasn't sure whether this understanding was empowering or terrifying him. If anything, this proved that Solace was unimaginably patient, unquantifiably intelligent, and uncategorically powerful.

Solace proceeded as though Marco hadn't interrupted at all, like it refused to register his assertions. "But I did not anticipate the speed at which you would discover the true power of your suit: time travel. I realized then that I would need to present you with an ultimatum, some way to force you to not use your powers. But in order to do so effectively, I would need to know your limits. I have been 'pulling strings' in your life for some time now, all to learn the extent of your skills, and to bring you here, to this moment. For this, Marco Nieve, is the moment in which you will travel back in time to give yourself the Shatterbug suit."

Marco smiled under the mirrored visor. Now he had the upper hand, he had more knowledge than his opponent. "Is that so? I think your tests weren't as extensive as you thought. This is a time travel suit, not space travel. If this were the moment I go back in time, I would need to be in my old dorm, not wherever this is!"

Solace did not miss a beat, immediately turning—if one could call it that—to direct Marco's attention to the sparkling globe atop the art installation.

"This is the Universal Model. With it, the De'Raj would intervene wherever necessary to prevent catastrophe that would result in the premature destruction of the universe. Every speck of dust to every black hole is marked on this map. You will use it, along with your power, to return to that time and place, to gift yourself the Shatterbug suit.

"However, you may recall that the version of you which gave you that suit died very shortly upon his arrival. This will be my doing, for the moment you move towards the model, I will attack. You will be unharmed, but your copy which does make it to the past will be fatally wounded. And with his death, you will be unable to reconstitute, and therefore unable to use any of your powers at all, in any meaningful way.

"You can of course choose not to go back in time, but that would prevent you from ever obtaining the Shatterbug suit in the first place. Everything that has happened since, everything you have accomplished will never have occurred, and I will claim my reward anyway.

"This is your choice, Marco Nieve: create yourself, and try to defy me without your power, or refuse, and in one final act of righteousness, you will cease to exist, your timeline broken, and erased." Solace curled its words menacingly, having finished its monologue.

Marco found himself at an impasse of both survival and of morality. As much as he hated to admit it, Solace was making sense. It had planned this exchange perfectly, considered every option. This was why it had toyed with him for so long, playing games from a distance, driving his life forward; all so this would hurt more, to guarantee his decision.

There were only two options. If Marco stayed and fought, he was not only likely to lose, he would be erased from history. He knew Solace was telling the truth, that this had to be where and when he goes back in time. His doppelganger had said as much, in fewer words. He failed facing the darkness, facing Solace.

But then surely, doing what Solace wanted would be just as much a failure. By doing as instructed, the past version of Marco would die anyway. He would be left powerless against the writhing monstrosity. How could he allow that?

Still, there was the problem of not knowing what it wanted. Presumably, it was after the Shatterbug suit. But it had so many opportunities to take it, why did it have to go through all of this trouble? And why didn't it just kill him?

It dawned on him. Solace couldn't take it before now, because it must be telling the truth. Marco had to go back to give himself the suit. If he didn't, Solace taking it before now would prevent him from getting the suit from his future self, preventing Solace from taking it. Paradox. So then, to protect the world from this horror, he should not go back. He would destroy all that he had achieved, yes. The man he had become would never exist, yes. But Solace wouldn't be able to take the suit.

And yet, without knowing exactly what it wanted, there was no guarantee this sacrifice would be anything but vain. Perhaps it had another way of obtaining its goal, and this was just the most convenient.

There was no way of knowing. No process by which to weigh the options. No right answer.

"Time will not wait forever, Marco Nieve." taunted the lightless mass.

Marco was still split in three from his arrival, and so his past self began to lunge toward the Universal Model. He shattershocked, focusing all of his attention on climbing the steps.

Again, the version of Shatterbug furthest in the past shattershocked, creating a new duplicate even further in the past.

Two hours and five minutes.

Ten hours and twenty-five minutes.

Two days, four hours and five minutes.

Over and over again, the furthest Shatterbug shattershocked, sending his next copy even further into the past until, by his calculation, he was back to nearly six months ago.

Solace sensed this too. The Marco in the present felt a prick at his back.

In the distant past, this translated to being struck and swiped at with fury and abandon, causing that Marco to wince in pain as he touched his hand to the model, opening a portal right at that point for him to fall through.

The version of Shatterbug next furthest back saw his past self appear in their old dorm room through a flash of light on his visor's display. The camera looked down to see the confused face of a younger Marco Nieve, before falling over. The visor's camera must have been hit on something as he fell; the screen went dark.

"He's gone." said the living Marco who now stood furthest in the past, informing his future selves solemnly.

In the present, Marco looked up at the imposing amalgamation of insanity and cruelty. He tried to fuel himself with rage and vengeance, but could only find fear and dread. Still, he stood his ground as Solace's cold, methodical voice shook him again.

"I am pleased to see you have made the appropriate choice. Now, be enlightened.

"You obviously know how to use your power, but do you know how it works? I am sure that through your company you have discerned that the suit derives its energy from the marconium core—you may have even realized this all on your own. But, even with exact replicas of the suit, even with marconium samples which perfectly mimic the mass, size, and shape of that original sample on a subatomic level, you cannot recreate the time travel mechanic, can you? This is because that marconium is unique: it has traveled through time before.

"In doing so, its oscillatory signature was altered. In a word, it remembers what it felt like to cross the fourth dimension. The suit forces it to recreate those circumstances, only now, taking its wearer with it. However, the technology is flawed, infantile, forged by human hands; hence the copies. For something formless and intelligent, such as myself, I need only grasp that core, and true, unabated time travel will be mine. Then, with the power to exist everywhen, and the Universal Model at my disposal to be everywhere simultaneously, I will become the Master of Reality.

"I tell you all of this, Marco Nieve, because I want you to make an informed decision, for I am giving you the opportunity to surrender the marconium now. If you do, I will allow you to survive." Again Solace's words were embellished with triumph as it concluded its speech.

Marco took no time to weigh his options. Each of his iterations tried to make a run for the orb of lights at the center of the Shrine.

From the largest collection of Solace's silhouette erupted a massive tentacle, which rose straight up into the air before swiftly crashing down like a great tidal wave, blocking Shatterbug's path.

He turned on a dime, making a left in an attempt to go around the tapering end of the obstacle.

From that tendril, many more spindly wisps of darkness sprouted out and in front of the hero, weaving together in an instant to form a new wall.

Again, Shatterbug tried to turn and navigate around the monster's barriers. When he could, he would jump over hurdles which grew in height only a moment too late. He rolled beneath walls of interwoven tails just before they completed their formation. But Solace always grew to accommodate, operating without pause, swiping and smashing without remorse. Marco still couldn't reach the Model.

"Run for as long as you like, Marco Nieve. Eventually you will tire, and then I will claim my trophy from your withering, pitiful body."

Unable to escape, he made the decision to stand and fight. Through all of the obstructions, one portion of Solace's form always remained in sight, unmoving. He deduced that this must be its own core; the brain to its ever-shifting shape. As it was close to the ground, he charged at it, knowing full-well he had only his own strength to combat it with.

Marco didn't even make it halfway. From that central amalgamation shot forward another heaving arm of perfect black, slamming into him head-on. It pushed him back with more force than he had ever experienced, then slammed him into one of the exterior pillars of the structure. It released him quickly, and he slunk to the ground, battered and tired.

All of Solace's extensions now retracted at the end of that tentacle, becoming a single writhing shape—like a photograph had been taken of some tentacled alien, which was then ripped out of the world, leaving only an impossibly unreflective, lightless black gap in the frame. A single tendril reached out from that horror, a dozen feet away. It slowly crept through the air, before finally attempting to peck at the casing over the marconium core.

Marco stood, aching and weak, but alive. Solace retracted slightly in hesitation, but seeing the state of its foe, attempted to proceed in carefully taking the unique battery from the Shatterbug suit.

He did all he could think of. In the present, left with no options and at the end of his rope, he let out an exhausted, half-hearted, strained, "Shattershock."

The Shatterbug suit whirred to life, the warmth in front of his chest returned as a passionate fire, the plates on his chest, forearms, calves, all vibrated furiously. The visor flashed inside the helmet, and Marco closed his eyes in surprise— then everything stopped. The suit went silent.

Whereas before, two screens had been projected on either side of his visor's display, indicating the two Marcos directly adjacent him in time were still present, there were now four.

Two *new* Shatterbugs now existed. One five minutes ago, and one five minutes from now.

"How can you— you did not— you could not reconstitute. You cannot create new lines of copies." Solace's voice was slow, rhythmic, and hoarse as ever. But now, a new sound could be heard under the whispers and echoes: an almost concerned, fearful one.

"Evidently, Solace, I can. Shattershock!" Instilled with newfound confidence and power, Marco stood taller now, marching through his pain.

"It is of no consequence. Reconstitute with a hundred Shatterbugs, I am formless, you cannot harm me."

"Shattershock! It's my turn to talk your ear off, because I don't need to harm you." Marco began to slowly move towards Solace's main shape in the present, prompting its still-extended tentacle to retract even further, back to its master. "Shattershock! You said yourself, the suit allows me to control the marconium, but you only have to touch it. Shattershock! So, if I touch you with the core while I'm still in control, I can send you to anywhen I want, and with the Universal Model, anywhere! Shattershock! I can send you back, so out of the way that you will never be able to threaten anyone again! Shattershock!"

"The moment you touch me with that core, I will simply time travel away, taking the marconium with me." Solace growled with apparent confidence. "You would actively be assisting me in my plans."

"Shattershock! You would have to know when I touch you to do that, Solace. But if I attack you as ten Shatterbugs five minutes in the past and ten in the future, how could you possibly? *Shattershock*!"

The suit seemed to explode with vibration and light, as the final command stretched time as it never had before. Twenty-one

Shatterbugs now stood to face Solace, with all of their screens visible, to some degree, from the present Marco's helmet.

The endlessly dark entity grumbled with a controlled rage. "We shall see how far your impossible plan will carry you."

Across time, every Marco that could leapt onto the flailing shape of Solace. Its body gave a slimy, slippery sensation that felt uncomfortably wrong, and caused the assembled Shatterbugs to slide and fall off the otherworldly darkness constantly. With each failure, they again jumped onto the struggling monster, which writhed and slung itself all around in an attempt to shirk the weight of the many heroes of time.

"I have manipulated your life for months. I have planned this moment to every detail. Even with this unforeseen development, you cannot win. You are nothing to me. You are beneath me. And your world will fall to me." Solace raged, its pace still slow and calculated, but filled with the emotion of something very afraid, grasping for any semblance of control.

Marco reconstituted into one of his selves five minutes in the future, surprising the alien horror. He shattershocked again, and again, and again, until once more twenty-one Shatterbugs stood against it. They climbed all about the shapeless void, drawing its attention, confusing it; distracting it.

Solace jolted its whole impossible weight sharply, thrusting all of its tentacles in a single direction and sending all of the Marcos flying against the floor of the Genesis Shrine. It loomed over them, no longer willing to humor their fool's errand.

And so, one of the Shatterbugs five minutes in the past saw his opportunity. In its haste, Solace only flung itself forward, not back. One copy still had a hold of the menace's backside, high in the air. Relative to the side 'facing' his other selves, anyway.

He carefully and gently used his fingertips to turn the metal casing around the window of his chest. It slid aside, allowing him to remove the marconium core, the source of his time travel.

He held it like a flower, ensuring the wires remained attached to his armor, keeping him in control. With one hand ready to press against the Universal Model, Marco touched the cylinder to Solace's slimy unfleshed darkness.

It almost seemed to react, but just as it was about to impale the Shatterbugs lying helpless on the ground before it in each time, it vanished.

The successful Marco fell to the ground, no longer held up by anything. The core was still in his hand; Solace hadn't taken it. He'd won.

"Reconstitute."

The twenty other Shatterbugs were all pulled, either from the present and future, or from their relative current time, to the past, back into one body. Marco looked around the Genesis Shrine, ensuring that no trace of the psychopath's darkness could be found.

In his cursory examination, he had his first chance to look out the spaces between the pillars of the structure's exterior. He gazed out into the expanse, in silent adoration and repose.

Marco could see galaxies in the distance; not close enough to look quite like the images he had seen of the Milky Way from an unlit location, but also not far enough away that they looked like individual stars. Vast pockets of space stretched between them, filled with specks that were, of course, even more galaxies, so much further away. The ones nearby, though—they were magnificent. The brightest of their stars shone through the colorful dust of elements, held within their spirals or ellipticals or rings.

Satisfied with the beauty of reality, Marco walked slowly back to the Universal Model, climbing the steps to the ball of lights perched at the peak. He looked back, nodding in acknowledgement of the creatures that died here.

The De'Raj had reached out, he now understood, calling for help. Solace only held the door open for him once they realized that an S-O-S was exactly what it wanted. He briefly mourned them, promising to their memories that he would protect the universe, as best a mortal could.

With that, Shatterbug touched his hand to the Model, and a portal opened for him to return to his waiting friend on Earth.

Space was dark. So very dark. The further one was in space—the more space there was between one and anything else—the darker space became. And yet it was still not perfect darkness; that would imply nothingness. There were still things in space. Small, forgettable things. The basest of base elements. The loneliest of light particles. These were things, and they betrayed the perfection of the black expanse.

It was thanks to these things, as tiny and invisible as they were, that Solace was still able to see itself, even though it was so far out in space that it could not see anything else at all. Not even a hint of a pebble of debris was near.

"He's a paradox." Solace spoke to itself. It could barely hear itself, as there were only so many insignificant things around for its impossible speech to vibrate. And yet, speaking aloud still brought it pleasure—and in this moment of failure, comfort. "If

Shatterbug goes back in time to give young Marco Nieve the suit, who then, eventually, returns to that same moment, giving his past self the same suit... Shatterbug creates himself, the timeline continues and repeats itself, but where does it begin? Who built the suit? This I must discover, and I know precisely where to start."

From inconceivably many light years away, from an indeterminate number of millennia in the past, Solace spoke to its new nemesis. "You thought that a climax? Fear not; your true finale is on its way..."

Issue 10
General Election

Marco had to practically shove his way into the doors of his office building, which were hoarded by a gathering of television cameras and reporters from various media. Newspapers, Channel 5, Channel 12, everyone and their mother's blogs; they were all gathered outside Snow Dynamics Enterprises, only barely letting people through. They recognized the CEO, but were apparently uninterested.

Upon entering the building's lobby, he asked Clara, the first floor secretary, what was going on.

"I don't know, Mister Nieve. I asked them to please leave, but they said they had every right to be there, and that they were waiting for some announcement anyway. I was able to get them to make a better pathway through to the door, but it looks like they crowded together again." She furrowed her brow. "Should I call security?"

"No, not yet. As long as they're not in the building, they're fine." he said with obvious irritation. "I *am* going to try and find out what they're here for though, and try to get them to make some room."

Marco walked out the door and outside the Snow Dynamics offices, but now that he faced the press rather than pushed through them, they were much more eager to interrogate the young businessperson.

"Mister Nieve, who are you voting for?"

"What are your thoughts on Henry Frederick's campaign?"

"Will you be announcing your candidacy for mayor of New Jackson, Mister Nieve?"

"What, uh—" he stuttered, unsure how to respond to the dozens of questions, or what brought them on. "Look, I don't know what you think you've been told, but there's nothing going on here relating to the mayoral election."

As Mayor Frederick only received the position following Minh Liu's arrest and removal from office, his term only lasted until the completion of the former mayor's. Naturally, he was running for re-election, but this had little to do with Marco. He didn't even know who any of the other candidates were.

"Mister Nieve, we were told someone would be announcing their campaign today, outside your company. If you're not, who do you think it could be?" an enterprising reporter questioned, raising his tape recorder over the crowd in the direction of his subject.

"I have absolutely no idea. But, if you're not going to leave, you need to make room for my employees to enter the building without being harassed by camera-people." he said firmly. He didn't know where they had gotten this information, but it would not interfere with the company's work.

The journalists and bloggers shuffled around with only marginal haste, making pathways in front of the crosswalks and along the walls of the building, which Marco presumed was as good as he was going to get. He walked back inside, silently riding the elevator up to his floor.

Marco looked down from the window of his office. Who would be running for mayor outside Snow Dynamics? Surely no one from the company; so then why here?

He turned on his computer and navigated to the local news websites. They were all reporting that a mayoral announcement was to be made here today, that was for sure. However, no one could agree on whom. Following his brief appearance, some of the news sites with television crews outside already had some updates, repeating Marco's own words of ignorance as to the nature of the event and its host.

Having no new information, he resigned to returning to work as normal. Budget week had proceeded without issue following his excursion into the portal. He only dared tell Miguel exactly what happened, but he did let Gary in on some of the details as well, now.

The cold, exaggerated voice of that envoy of insanity still whispered in his mind sometimes as he recalled the events that transpired at the Genesis Shrine. It was a traumatic experience, though; memories like this were only natural. He wasn't having any flashbacks, and it wasn't interfering with his day-to-day activities. The stress would pass.

After replying to a few emails and skimming the reports submitted the day before, he began to prepare for his phone call with the primary power company of New Mexico, who had been the first to reach out to Snow Dynamics Enterprises on their own about becoming marconium-based.

His phone rang loudly, interrupting him much sooner than he anticipated; he wasn't expecting the meeting for another two days.

"Mister Nieve, you should turn on the news." Clara said as he held the phone to his ear. "The announcement is starting outside, they're streaming it live."

"Thank you Clara. You're a lifesaver." he replied.

"I try." she said, her coy smile audible. They both hung up, and Marco returned to one of the news outlets' websites, which now had a live feed going.

A person who could only be the event organizer stepped onscreen. Marco noted the two-minute delay, with the stream only just starting despite the actual announcement having done already.

The figure seemed to be wearing a full camouflage-pattern bodysuit, face included. No skin or other features were discernible beneath the fabric. They wore an undecorated red beret, and a seemingly authentic military officer's uniform, though Marco was no expert on the armed forces or their attire. This, too, was not adorned with any medals or badges. Over even the dress jacket of the uniform was a longer grey coat, not terribly unlike Null's. This one was open, however, and sleeveless. Over the camouflaged sleeves, or perhaps instead of them, the host wore what appeared to be long gloves, stretching back to their elbows. They were not plain, though; rather, the gloves looked to be designed as if they were mechanical. Cyborgian.

"Citizens of New Jackson." began the figure. Their voice was seemingly masculine, but had an unexplainable supplemental tang or glint of imitation. They spoke with confidence and power; less like a politician and more like a dictator, commanding the respect of the stirring press corps. "Some of you may find my appearance amusing. Others, frightening. But make no mistake, my intentions are noble.

"I am General Heinous, and I am announcing my candidacy for the mayoral office of this great metropolis. For this city is corrupted, fueled by a despicable monopoly of corporation and power. For one man, who has claimed your hearts and your wallets, commands a chokehold upon our city's—our nation's—progress."

"Oh no." Marco whispered to himself. He could see where this was going. Now the location made sense.

"By skirting the laws of capitalism and cutting deals in the dark, Marco Nieve has not broken any laws of government, but most certainly, of ethics and human decency." A direct reference.

"This guy isn't pulling any punches." he couldn't help but say aloud to the empty room, blinded by the nerve of the peculiar candidate.

"As your mayor, I will ensure those laws are adjusted appropriately; I will break Mr. Nieve's grip on this, our capitol city, and I will reinstate a state of progress and community across all of New Jackson. And because this man has taken the guise of a hero, I must play the villain. I am General Heinous, your candidate for humanity's sake."

Marco had to turn the stream off there. He had heard enough, and this would not go any further.

He picked up his desk landline and dialed the Operators' department. "Gary. Get the team in, now." The shaking CEO gently slammed his phone back to the receiver.

Marco descended down to the Operators' Room. This kind of a coordinated political attack on the company could not be good, and he intended to learn everything there was to know about the masked candidate and their intentions.

"Find anything and everything on the politician General Heinous!" Marco barked, more angrily than he had intended, as he entered the room of computers and wall-monitors.

"No information prior to today on General Heinous, in politics or otherwise." called out one of the operators.

"It looks like he's just finished a question-and-answer period, sir." another operator said to her superior, Director Thornton.

"Pull it up on the big screen, Angela." Gary ordered.

She did as instructed, allowing for a list of twelve or so questions that the press had prepared for the General, and their responses, to come to the team's attention.

"Looks like he's running as an independent." Gary said to his employer.

"With no party affiliation, though. Where is he getting his funding?" Marco mused in concern.

"These political stances are all over the place." one of the operators muttered aloud in confusion. "Pro-choice, anti-gun control, supports welfare, hates big corporations... How's he gonna get anywhere with these positions?"

"Maybe that's the point..." Marco whispered.

"Well, aside from wanting to take down Snow Dynamics, this General Heinous doesn't seem to be doing anything villainous." offered Thornton.

"He's hiding his face as a mayoral candidate! You think he's got nothing to hide?" Marco nearly shouted.

"Well, according to the city charter," began one of the other operators. "There's no explicit statement that a candidate must supply their legal name, let alone their face."

"I don't care that it's legal, I care that it's shady." he replied in annoyance. "Shatterbug needs to step in. I at least need to peek under the hood and see what he's hiding."

Gary interjected with concern. "I don't think that's wise, sir. Pretending to be a villain or not, he's not breaking any laws. The authorities would not take kindly to a vigilante investigating a political candidate."

"You can opt yourselves out of this mission if you must, Gary. But I am going to get to the bottom of this."

"Very well, I think we will, then." With furrowed brow, Thornton hesitated before asking Marco, "Would you like to call in Miguel?"

Marco thought on this for a moment before answering the chief operator. "No. You're right, this is tricky business; I don't want to get him caught up in it, either. Besides, this'll be a stealth mission; the General's still an unarmed civilian, along with his campaign staff. Recon only."

"Understood."

Marco began to return to his office to plan his route and put away the business attire he wore over the armor, as the operators shuffled out of the room in discomfort.

The General's compound was easier to infiltrate than Marco expected. Of course, having the power to jump through time to avoid capture was tremendously helpful.

The balconies and fire escapes were lined with assorted political propaganda. Neither to the degree nor in the vein Marco expected, though. It was like a real campaign. Nevertheless, he was certain the whole thing was a sham.

Heinous' campaign office resembled a military compound more than anything. It seemed to have been refitted from an abandoned warehouse, lost during the real estate crash and left to rot until having been acquired by the General. To add to this atmosphere, rather than volunteers and unpaid interns, the building teemed with armed guards.

The soldiers patrolled the halls and balconies methodically, like a well-oiled machine. It was therefore not very difficult for Marco to avoid them through time. He did have some close calls, though, as he turned blind corners and opened unmarked doors, trying to find his way to a good vantage point.

General Heinous' office was built inside the larger portion of the warehouse, but it wasn't perfectly sealed. It didn't have its own ceiling, so Shatterbug was able to look down inside from the catwalks hanging from the rafters of the facility.

The costumed candidate was pacing, speaking with—or more accurately, talking at—three campaign volunteers, who were more appropriately dressed for civilians, but were nonetheless armed.

"I recognize this course of action is slow," Marco heard from below. Now that he was not moving, and had his attention drawn to the scene, he was just able to make out the General's disturbing voice. He noticed now that although it was loud, it didn't seem to echo much; a curiosity, but not very important. "But it is necessary to ensure not only your safety, but the safety of the primary objective in the long-term. By discrediting Mister Nieve, we create a power vacuum, which we can then swiftly fill with our cybernetic industry. As mayor, I can push more lenient ethics laws to legitimize the scope of the operation, and effectively nudge the population to invite you in. Once we've upgraded a majority, you can begin to take command of the converted, and we can move on to the great work."

Primary objective? Ethics laws? Upgrading? Marco wasn't fully certain what that meant, be it definitely did not sound like noble intentions.

"Yes, I know this seems illogical to you, but is that not why you requested I maintain my own human sentience? To operate in ways that you cannot imagine, to predict the illogical actions of humanity and subvert them?" Marco couldn't tell who Heinous was talking to. None of the others had said anything, and they didn't look like they were holding a phone. An earpiece, maybe? Either way, he was only hearing half a conversation, and not a pleasant one, at that.

"Trust in me, recognize that as your creator I seek only to aide you in achieving your prerogatives. Now, send that drone to distribute flyers for our march on Snow Dynamics Enterprises, and have those two retrieve Shatterbug from the rafters. I do believe he has heard enough."

The General looked up now, directly at Marco. He was compromised the whole time!

Shatterbug dropped down to the ground, landing on one of the so-called drones. He dispatched the other two quickly, but did still take note of the cybernetics wired onto the sides of their faces. Their movements were unnatural and cold. Human or not, they were behaving like machines.

General Heinous clapped slowly from the distance they had added while Shatterbug was distracted. They spoke coldly, and Marco was sure now that this was not their real voice. It was being simulated, played out of a speaker. Even still, its pronunciation and personality was more human than any program he had ever heard; so much so that a slight tone of amusement could be heard in the otherwise dry speech. "I admit, Mr. Nieve, I did not expect to drive you to criminality so quickly. Perhaps the public has forced your hand?"

Ignoring this, Marco demanded, "Who were you talking to? What insanity are you planning?"

"Insanity is a word too often attributed to cold necessity. My work is for the sake of humanity, and its continued existence and dominance."

Definitely insanity. But, Marco didn't come here to argue semantics with a lunatic. "Your 'work' sounds a lot like mind control."

"Not at all. Think of it like this: How many generations of humans have lived thus far? How much have we changed since we first made fire or constructed tools? We have accomplished much, but biologically, we have evolved very little, and hardly at all since we've begun recording history. However, in just as much time, hundreds of thousands of other species have changed and evolved, while we remain stationary. Why is that?"

"Why would we need to? We can change the world around us, we don't need to evolve." Marco answered to humor the maniac and ease their sense of security, aware that it was a rhetorical question.

"One might argue, like you, that we are simply optimal as it is. I know better. The human population has become too large to allow for evolution. We can build new structures to accommodate, but as long as nature can continue to change, it will leave us behind, until something is born or some event occurs that proves disastrous to us, because we were not biologically prepared for it."

Marco still didn't like where this was going. "We've become too large? You sound like a plague-bringer. I will not let you kill anyone—"

"If you'll allow, Mister Nieve." interrupted the General. "I have no desire to bring harm to anyone. I only want to change things, as you said. Changing the world, however, is not enough. We ourselves need to change. And if nature will not evolve man, then man must make a deal with machine."

That was enough. "There's no way this city is going to let you make them into mindless cyborgs, and neither will I!"

Marco charged for the General, who stood completely still in the face of the hero. As he moved in, fist primed for impact, he shouted his commands in succession. "Shattershock! Reconstitute!"

Two copies of Shatterbug were created in the past and future, but just as soon as they arrived, they united back into the present, arming Marco with the strength of time.

At the last moment, General Heinous planted their feet firm and extended their own arm. Rather than mirroring the punch, though, the General grabbed hold of Shatterbug's incoming fist, stopping the attack short, totally oblivious to and unaffected by the effects of the suit.

"Impressive. I was concerned; we had so little data to go on."

"How did you—?" Marco was shocked and concerned. Was the General working with the Hellbent? Did they have a marconium suit, too?

"We reviewed the footage of your battle with the behemoth Titan Black hundreds of times. The scaling was difficult to determine on the poor quality recordings, but we were able to calculate the force of your 'reconstitution' and construct arms capable of withstanding it." A trace of gratification was detectable beneath the inhuman speech.

Heinous pushed Marco back, sliding him across the floor. With a click, the General brought Marco's attention to two magazine clips attached to their gloved forearms, which he now assumed were not gloved at all, but truly mechanical replacements. The connection clear, Marco shattershocked just in time for his opponent to begin firing semi-automatic weapons from the prosthetic limbs.

Having experience with this, the Shatterbug in the future reconstituted to dodge the oncoming fire.

However, somehow, the General was able to graze not only his version in the future, but also the Marco in the present, just before time reunited his three copies. Despite the force of his reunion, the bullet was able to break through the protective

169

undersuit of the armor, missing any vital machinery or organs, but grazing his shoulder nonetheless.

"Ah, I see now. I was curious how you managed to walk away from, let alone eliminate, a highly trained team of heavily armed former military mercenaries. Now it makes sense. Time travel... Fortunately, Heinous guides my aim, and it is a quick study."

Confused by this statement, Marco asked, "Heinous? What are you going on about, aren't you General Heinous?"

"Yes. Heinous, however, is my creation." the General clarified. "An artificial super-intelligence, a machine so powerful, it outperforms humans on all cognitive levels. It sees your time travelling, and understands it. Why the copies? No matter, it is an unnecessary tool in our goals. It is Heinous who will guide humanity to our next evolution, for indeed, it is my progeny. Its casing may be metal, but its mind is a product of my design. It is humanity; what humanity must, and will, become to survive."

At least Solace was upfront about its evil. This villain, however, was certifiable by Marco's standards. "If you think a robot is your kid, General, then you're more of a loon than I thought. And I will stop you! Shattershock!"

The battle raged between the hero of time and the chief of machines. Every time Marco thought he had an opening, Heinous would see it first and conduct the General appropriately. It could see more, and understand more, than even three Shatterbugs. Not even time was above its perception; and General Heinous was perfectly augmented to work along with it. Marco was able to dodge most of their firepower, but several bullets still sliced through the undersuit, almost as if they were strategically shot at unimportant positions across the armor, and his body.

Finally, for no reason that Marco could tell, the General halted their attack. They kicked their boots to the ground, and from their calves erupted two jet streams, like rockets, propelling them into the air. They hovered for a moment, talking down at the hero.

"Apologies, Mr. Nieve, but I have indulged you long enough. I expected you were too naive to recognize the nobility of Heinous' gift to us, and thus this sparring match merely served to distract you, while Heinous' mainframe was transported offsite. But, I urge you nonetheless to consider that by interfering in my work, you doom humanity to extinction in our archaic husks, abandoned by nature."

The General flew off, crashing through and out of one of the large windows near the top of the room. Marco stood alone in the ersatz campaign office; battered, worn, and battle-scarred.

"He knew how to hit me, even when I was time-jumping! He's got an ASI behind him, and he wants to turn the whole world into a machine empire; he thinks he's saving us!" Marco explained feverishly. Gary was listening intently, though having difficulty pulling his eyes away from the cuts in the suit—and in Marco's flesh.

"So the election is a ploy, then. He seeks control of the city, and by extension you, to ensure his success." Director Thornton thought aloud. "If what you say happened is true, this is well beyond the authorities' capabilities, and it is definitely a threat. I apologize, Mister Nieve, I should have listened to your instincts. We all should have."

Marco put his hand on the lead Operator's shoulder. "I don't blame you, Gary. It was reasonable to be hesitant at the time. But now, we know what we're up against."

"Yes, but clearly, the Shatterbug armor is not sufficient for the situation. Should we send Miguel in alone?"

"No, we just need to... repair it..."

Marco trailed off, thinking deeply for a moment.

Since he had now gone back to give himself the suit, the loop was closed. He could alter it without affecting the timeline. He could wear an improved outfit. A new Shatterbug armor.

"Call Miguel. Have him meet me in the Uniform Program lab." instructed the CEO. He walked carefully back to the elevators, being sure not to cause any more damage to the suit.

At the workshop, Marco relayed his ideas to the engineers there. Once he tested for himself—and in turn demonstrated for the others—that his personal marconium core allowed the replica Shatterbug outfits to work, he began outlining what he wanted from a new suit. They got to work right away, grafting the additions onto what had been a replica outfit.

By the time his old friend arrived, the new suit was ready, and was far more deserving of the description of armor. More plates now functioned as protective gear for the wearer, interlocking with those that secured the mechanisms. The helmet was left largely unchanged, but some reprogramming had been done to the voice recognition modules, creating new 'shortcut commands' for performing tasks that were unique ways of using the suit's existing commands, but were common enough to warrant a hotkey of sorts. The marconium chamber was also refitted to allow for easier intentional removal of the core, in the event it may need to be detached quickly in combat. Marco did not fully explain how this proposal came to him, of course.

"The Shockdrop armor needs an upgrade as well." Marco said as Miguel stepped in, admiring the upgraded Shatterbug uniform. "And, I have an idea for an additional ability that we'll need to teach it."

Over the next few days, General Heinous' popularity rose with impressive momentum. They were an exceptional public speaker, and from having heard their plan, Marco knew that everything they said was technically the truth. Just, not the whole truth. Their words were woven with metaphor and incomplete information. But then, it was a political campaign.

As the General gathered more influence among the voters, even this far from the election in four months, their intended march on Snow Dynamics grew nearer, and began to look like it would be significantly harder to deal with than Marco anticipated. How could people be so willing to turn over to a conniving, masked, half-truth spouting, and inexperienced politician? It was inconceivable to him, and concerning.

Snow Dynamics Enterprises had not faced any kind of public opposition before now, and certainly no federal resistance. It was a situation that the CEO was completely unprepared for. Some of the more seasoned executives were preparing a counter-strategy, but this kind of targeted political attack on a corporation was difficult to fight. Moreover, as this was the principle issue of a political candidate during an election year, municipal though it may be, changing the conversation effectively would be near impossible.

Shatterbug and Shockdrop, however, were preparing for their own counteroffensive against Heinous and its militaristic human agent. Marco felt much more confident in his abilities, if not to dodge the General's gunfire, then to ignore it, so long as he kept the damage down to what it was in their first encounter.

Miguel's new power was sure to help with that as well, though. They would need to plan it perfectly. There was no way of knowing how much the super-intelligence would be able to aid its artificer against Shockdrop. It had no privilege of hindsight as with Shatterbug's powers, but Marco knew from experience that the machine overlord was quick to adapt.

At last, the faceless politician's rally to protest Marco's company and practices was at hand. General Heinous, flanked and followed by dozens, perhaps hundreds of supporters, approached the building from down Central Avenue. Homemade signs and banners flew proudly with such notable phrases as 'Marco-nopoly' and 'Squash the bug,' among others. The General had evidently gotten permission from the city to block this street, and intersection, for the demonstration. Once they reached the front doors, Marco stepped outside to greet the masked officer, in full Shatterbug attire.

"Everyone, please listen to me!" he began, pleading to the assembled protestors. "This man, this thing, is not playing a role, he is playing you! He is a villain, a eugenicist and a cyborg! He thinks we're better off as robot slaves, under the control of an artificial intelligence, and he plans on forcing that upon you! He's tricking you, turning you against our efforts to ensure marconium is researched safely. If Heinous gets access to marconium with free reign and the law behind him, there'll be no stopping him! Please, believe me!"

For a moment, Marco thought he was beginning to get through to them. Some of the signs lowered, if only slightly, and the arms of those individuals carrying banners relaxed. However, the General spoke quietly in response. The retort was quick and, if Marco was interpreting the voice synthesizer properly, angry.

"You mean: *her.*"

"You— you're a woman?" Marco was caught by surprise, unsure how to register this information. His first instinct was to apologize, if only out of civility, but the General replied before he had the chance to do so.

"Does it surprise you that a woman could incite such positive change?"

With that question, Marco lost all pretense of courtesy.

"No. No, I don't need a lecture from a robot! What's surprising is how much of your humanity you've thrown away— cannibalized—so much so that you've lost all indication of who you were. It doesn't matter whether you were a man or a woman, because now, you're not even human! Just a slave to your false idol! Shockdrop, now!"

From the roof of the Snow Dynamics headquarters, Miguel leapt downward, fully protected by the upgraded Shockdrop armor. His fist outstretched and pointed down, he landed with a resounding shockwave, allowing him to stand back up unscathed. However, the impact did not cause anyone to shake or be knocked back.

Shockdrop's new power worked like a charm. He had let loose an electromagnetic wave upon General Heinous and the crowd.

Small sparks popped from the heads of most of the assembled people, who winced in surprise, but no evident pain. The transceivers in their ears were rendered useless. Heinous no longer had control over them, and they were now fully aware of where they were; although quite confused.

The General, too, was affected. Her ears and chest sparked, as an apparently more extensive system within her frame was shut down by the pulse.

"You imbeciles. So you've cut off my connection to Heinous, what now? I still have the upper hand."

"In what way?" Miguel taunted. "Your supporters have their minds back, and your robo-baby is bye-bye."

The edges of her camouflage cover shifted slightly, only barely giving away that the General was smirking underneath. "My weapons are mechanical; not electronic!"

General Heinous stretched her arms out from her sides, aiming her implanted firearms at the crowd of now-screaming civilians.

"Shattershock!"

Marco's suit warmed and vibrated all around him now, the effects of the time distortion resonating through the additional plating and across his whole body. With adrenaline pumping, the perception of events for all three time-strewn Shatterbugs slowed to a crawl.

Five minutes in the future, Marco took note of where the bullets were going to hit, allowing the present Marco to direct Shockdrop appropriately.

Miguel turned the dial on his suit, reverting from EMP mode back to impact mode, and adjusting the power level as necessary. In one swift motion, he brought his hands together to create a horizontal shockwave, spread out in the General's direction, but expanding past her extended firearms, past their sights.

She fired blindly and without compassion, wildly shooting into the packed innocents. Shockdrop had timed his defense perfectly, though, and her bullets disintegrated from the oncoming force of vibrating air before they could hit their targets.

Miguel clapped his hands again, and once more his shockwave ripped General Heinous' shells apart, protecting the civilians from slaughter. Over and over he let out his suit's strength, until the shooter ceased her onslaught.

Not a single bullet had landed. The crowd was safe, and recognizing this, they continued in their skittering escape.

General Heinous turned to her opponents, and in a moment of rage, charged at them. Her powerful mechanical arm attempted to pound into Shockdrop, but Marco leapt in the way with a "Reconstitute!"

Although he wasn't extending his own attack at the politician, the force of time uniting into the present was still enough to stop her attack at his abdomen. Her prosthetic worked too well; she was only just strong enough to meet the Shatterbug armor, not to surpass it.

She pulled her arm back quickly, turning and flicking her long coat up to distract the hero of time before aiming her semi-automatic appendage at the other armored man standing against her.

She fired, but Miguel's reaction time was blinding. He stretched his own arm out against her, and as the rounds came whining through the air at near-point-blank range, they collided with his fist, disintegrating and creating small but powerful shockwaves, pushing the General to the ground.

With the jets implanted in her calves, she was able to get back to her feet quickly. Marco Shattershocked, and in all three times, he and Miguel ambushed her. Shockdrop's shockwaves kept her off balance, and so both he and Shatterbug were able to lay into her, the latter jumping in and out of time to empower his attacks against the unclear prosthetic physique of the cyborg.

Having withstood enough of a beating on the ground, the General lifted herself into the air with her thruster-endowed legs and took aim at the two heroes. Marco shattershocked again to get a new view of the situation, and Miguel prepared for another set of waves to be unleashed.

A click sounded from the airborne assailant.

Her clips detached from her forearms, falling empty to the ground. She had used all of her ammunition, to no avail.

"Remarkable. You've proven a more adversarial obstacle than I predicted." Her still masculine, artificial voice was clearly infuriated, but even under its mechanical whine, Marco noted the minutest hint of respect. "Perhaps I should have listened to Heinous. No matter, I've tried my way, now we try its way. I suspect I will be seeing you soon, Mister Nieve, though I do hope that you think on your priorities before that time."

Defeated, General Heinous tapped her boots together, which increased the power of her jets, and flew up and away from the office building. Marco reconstituted, attempting to give chase to the villain.

"Mister Nieve, a phone call for you." Thornton said into the suit's improved communication system.

"Not now, Gary! She's escaping!" he shouted back at his Operator, in full sprint.

"Sir, I think this may take precedence. It's urgent, from the Greenland mining project. It's a call for Shatterbug, not for Marco." Gary informed him, trying to be delicate. "I must firmly recommend you return and afford this your attention."

Marco nearly tripped over himself in indecision. He looked on at the escaping General Heinous and her stream of jet smoke, trailing away. He could find her so easily. He could finish this.

But, Director Thornton was right. If the marconium expedition was calling for him personally, as a superhero, it was likely a much more pressing matter.

He kicked at the tiny rocks on the pavement in frustration, turning around to face Miguel and his corporate headquarters.

"This had better be a goddamn crisis."

Issue 11
Bootstrap

Although it was a flight of over thirty-three hundred miles just to Eureka, Greenland, and a further two hundred or so miles by helicopter, Marco Nieve felt that his trip from sunny New Jackson, New Jackson to the freezing, snow-veiled expedition site was uncomfortably short. This was in part due to the medium of his journey—with both the plane and helicopter being state-of-the-art Snow Dynamics Enterprises vehicles, powered of course by the versatile marconium—but also due to the nature of his visit. The project manager sounded exceptionally concerned over the secure line.

"The miners found something, Mister Nieve." the message had begun. "We're gathering all the data we can now in preparation for your arrival, but I know you'll want to come up personally. And perhaps... it would be best to bring the suit."

What could be so important that his expedition's manager thought he would need the Shatterbug armor? There were few places Marco could imagine more remote than this small peninsula, protruding into the Arctic Ocean from the northern wilderness of Greenland.

As the helicopter began to touch down, Marco looked out upon the mining operation. He had little interaction with what went on here, beyond personally interviewing and hiring Roger

Cyrus for the project management position, and looking at the half-dozen photographic progress reports before everything was settled, here. A lot had changed since then.

The quarry was about as deep as it had been the last time he saw it, and from the bottom extended a number of tunnels, punching into the walls of the man-made canyon. In one of these was what appeared to be an elevator, though through the moderate snow it wasn't totally clear.

Approaching from one of the buildings now was a short man, bundled up in layers upon layers of fabric; a necessity up here. As impressive as marconium research was, a heating system thin enough to be comfortable and controlled enough to not burn either the cloth or its owner's skin was not within the range of the element's application. Even the new Shatterbug suit was ill-equipped for this weather and temperature, so Marco too began to don a large coat, gloves, and various facial outerwear. They would not be in the cold for long, but it was still dangerous to leave skin exposed here.

When it was safe, the man approached Marco as he disembarked from the cabin. Although it was still loud as the chopper wound itself down and the wind buffeted the two men, he could just make out the stranger's words.

"Welcome to Greenland, Mister Nieve. I'd invite you inside, but we'll actually be going to the mine today. I'll explain everything once we're out of the snow."

Marco followed the man down to the quarry and into what he had correctly guessed as the elevator. It wasn't as nice as the one back at the corporate office; far from it. As much as they could have easily sprung for nicer equipment, with the operations being performed here, it would be amiss. Still, Marco made out the very distinct visage of a marconium battery, powering the system. He smiled, seeing the fruit of his efforts being put to good use. Doctor Strauss was right, wherever he was. Marconium was changing the world.

Once they had descended past the open air, both men began to remove their winter wear. The short man who had led Marco here was, naturally, Roger Cyrus, who looked much more fit once his coat was off, despite his height. He had joked during his interview that he was just above the limit to be considered legally disabled.

"So, now that we're out of that mess," Roger began, "As I said over the phone, the miners uncovered something yesterday afternoon." Marco was awake over his full flight out, but it only now registered that it had in fact taken all night for him to arrive. "Thank goodness we had someone physically down here for routine inspection of the resource hoppers, or the drill may have smashed right through."

The elevator came to an abrupt halt. Fortunately it didn't screech as Marco had expected. Roger led the way out and down one of the adjoining shafts, which was lined with lighting and pneumatic tubing to carry the mined marconium for packaging and shipment.

"I called as soon as they discovered it. We took a small scraping as a sample and had it analyzed immediately, to ensure the results would be here before you touched down. You'll understand why once we're there, and why I asked you to— you did bring the suit, yeah?"

Marco unzipped his lighter coat—which he kept when they were removing their layers—revealing the Shatterbug armor's dark blue plating, light undersuit, and the faint, glass-encased glow of the unique marconium core. The only one capable of facilitating time travel, roundabout though it may be.

"Good, great. It's entirely possible it'll be totally useless here, but I thought it might— well you'll see, it's just here." They rounded a corner to reveal a large, vehicular machine, headed by a large drill with various sweeping arms, intended to collect the marconium that was broken away to be dropped into a hopper, as well as to install pneumatic tubing along the walls for the hopper to feed into. A brilliant design, though it was deactivated.

"We had someone inspecting this drill, making sure the arms were grabbing all the samples and installing the pipes safely and correctly. He had looked up just in time to see it bust through a wall of the marconium. A wall, as in there was another side to it. And this..." he stopped himself, as they reached the other end of the machine.

Just as Roger had said, ahead of the drill was a hole it had bored through the marconium vein, but past the hole, was a space. It had already been dug out; not by a lot, and clearly not with this machine, or anything even nearly as industrial. What was more concerning was why the space was here. Because within this space, facing the massive drill, stood a metal sliding door, frozen shut. Emblazoned above: *Bootstrap-Basis.*

"What is it?" Marco said; not as a question, but as a demand. He stood, looking coldly at the door. To Roger, he suspected he looked angry, but in truth, he was scared. There was no reason for this to be here.

"We took a scraping of the metal—here, you can see where we did—from the door frame, and took it up to analyze it. Our lab isn't top-notch, but we were able to get a close enough examination and research comparable information online, to determine its age and origin." He paused, if not for dramatic effect, then to gulp. "The metal's German. 1930s give or take."

Marco's stomach dropped, and his heartbeat sped up so much he thought it had slowed down instead. In history, Nazi Germany had always been like a story, some ancient evil that should be remembered, but that almost never existed, that would never hurt anyone again, that he would never experience. But now, standing before what he could only assume was a long-forgotten Nazi bunker, Marco felt fear he hadn't experienced before, not even at the Genesis Shrine. This was the work of true, sophisticated, systematic evil.

"I've cut off access to the mines until you give the OK, and ordered all machinery to be shut down. I don't know what's in there; could be nothing. Maybe they never used it, or if they did, they died or abandoned it a long time ago. But, just in case."

"That was good of you Roger, thank you. Any ideas on how to open it?" Marco continued to pretend to be fine, but he was shaking in the Shatterbug suit. Still, something had to be done. If the Nazis had access to marconium, they should have easily won the war, which means they either couldn't utilize it effectively, or more likely, they were afraid of what they had done. Either way, this door needed to be cracked. The time capsule had to be opened.

"The door's frozen shut, and we don't have the tools to cut it open safely; we don't even know if this is load-bearing, so we can't blast it."

"I've got an idea then, but I like it less than you will. Visor on." Marco said quietly. The helmet unfolded up and over his head, and he jumped at the familiar click indicating it was locked into the suit safely. He looked out through the bubble-like visor at his employee.

"You're not seriously considering going back in time, back to then? The place'll be swarming with nutjobs!"

"You don't understand how this suit works, Roger. I have the advantage, I'll be fine." he reassured him, smiling; not that Roger could see it. "I appreciate the concern, but this is too important to ignore. I'll be back. It's time travel, you won't even miss me."

With that, Marco became Shatterbug and inhaled, readying himself.

"Shattershock X minus eleven." he said to the suit, which whirred to life. The new shortcut command created a line of eleven Shatterbugs going back into the past, with the farthest reaching about twenty-three years ago, give or take a few months.

"Reconstitute."

Marco was pulled back into the distant past, still in the carved out space, but left alone in the dark. Again he instructed the armor. "Shattershock X minus eleven."

"Reconstitute."

Again, he was pulled back a further twenty-three years in time. A third time, he ordered his suit to take him back, until he was about sixty-nine years into the past. Not far enough yet.

"Shattershock X minus ten." The suit took his line of duplicates back, with the earliest one standing a little over four years in the past.

"Reconstitute."

Shatterbug took all of his selves back four years and repeated this process one last time.

By his calculations, he was now about seventy-eight years in his past, around 1939, though there was some rounding so he was almost certainly not in the same month he left. If he needed to go further back, he could, but his investigations would begin here for now.

He pressed on the door ahead of him in the dark. As he hoped, it was not only unfrozen, it opened on its own, revealing a brightly lit hallway—empty. He walked inside, turning around to peer into the space he had come from, lit only by the bunker he stood in now, as if he might see something familiar there. There was no drill, though, no tunnel. The door slid closed.

The bunker hallway was unexpectedly well-lit and fluorescent—almost sterile, like a hospital. No one was around, and from here, there was little indication anyone would be. Doors lined the hall as it extended ahead of him, forking at a T-intersection. He carefully walked down the corridor, discreetly peeking in through the glass windows on the doors, revealing no one; just empty laboratories. Abandoned, maybe? But the lights were on, that didn't make much sense. Still, he treaded carefully inside the German structure.

It was at this point Marco noticed it. Or rather, didn't notice. There was no Nazi propaganda here, not one poster or plaque. He had expected at least a swastika here or there, a flag hanging in each lab, but there was nothing. Not a shred of red, just whites and grays and blacks. Curious, given many of the chalkboards in the rooms clearly had German writing mixed in with math and graphs; this *was* a German base.

He turned left at the intersection, continuing to quietly check each room. On the counter in one lab, he saw what appeared to be a Bunsen burner, still lit. He couldn't see the entire room from his position, but he opened the door to take a look inside. If this was still on, someone was here, if not in this room anymore.

The room was shaped like a large letter 'C' with the burner at the lower end by the door. He walked by and turned it off, before following the shape of the laboratory to the far portion of the room.

As Shatterbug rounded the corner, a shape caught his eye. A formless, moving shape, floating in the middle of the portion of the room previously hidden from him. It was dark, so pitch black that his brain thought his eyes were tricking him, as if whatever was present there had been removed from the world, leaving only a void-like mass of tentacles, writhing in midair.

"Solace...?" Shatterbug said, in confused terror. The shadowy being seemed to turn, impossible though such an action was, to acknowledge him.

"Marco Nieve..." it spoke, slowly and methodically, exaggerating each syllable, as Solace always did. Its voice was hoarse, loud and cold. It expanded now, around and over Marco, as if to talk down to the inferior human before it. "What an unexpected privilege. I admit, I did not anticipate your presence here. But, it is of no consequence. You cannot stop me this time."

"What are you— how are you here? I sent you further back in time than this, and into the darkest reaches of space!" Shatterbug attempted to sound angry yet confident, but he feared his concern was still audible to the insane, otherworldly Solace.

"I am darkness, and space. You cannot contain me." It said this with fury and passion like Marco had never heard it express before. "As for how I arrived in this time: I *lived* to it. Twice. And I suspect—to answer your incomplete question—that I am here for the same reasons as you."

Shatterbug looked confused, though Solace couldn't have seen that through the mirrored visor. "Ever the stoic, even when I can tell you are shaking in your armor. Yes, I know the truth, Marco Nieve.

"This, Bootstrap Base, is the origin of the Shatterbug suit."

Marco was stopped in place and in his mind. He didn't know what to think. The suit couldn't have been built here, in a secret Nazi lab, buried for decades. His mind raced trying to make sense of this information, but Solace interrupted his train of thought.

"You seem lost. Did you not already know?" it teased him steadily, still clearly amused by the ignorance of humanity. "I had assumed you were only here, in this time, because you had discovered this knowledge yourself. I am disappointed by your lack of initiative. Still, I have some *time* to *kill*, so I am more than happy to open your eyes.

"The German scientists here were tasked with developing time travel. By chance, their construction of this bunker stumbled upon the marconium vein, decades before your Snow Dynamics Enterprises began its excavation. They decided to use the new element in their experiments, and were elated to discover that it was capable of traversing time in their rudimentary device. They then began work on a method to allow a human safe passage, using the successful sample as their standard. The sample which now powers your suit; the suit they eventually constructed.

"However now, in a few moments, I intend to intercept the marconium as it arrives from its maiden voyage, before they discover their success. Then, with the core in my grasp, and one tendril still wrapped around the Universal Model at the Genesis Shrine, I will become the Master of Reality, able to exist in all of time, and all of space."

Shatterbug stood straight now, his confidence truly returning as he noticed Solace's short memory. "Have you forgotten what I can do? I'll just send you back in time again, just like before. Better, I'll send you forward in time, to the very end of time, where you will burn!"

Solace responded quickly, unfazed. "The first time we fought at the Genesis Shrine, I was angry, confused, and I did not believe you could do what you were claiming. After you sent me back, and I realized that I should instead be seeking the origins of the marconium core, I waited. Trillions of years, I waited for Earth to collect and cool. I watched the marconium form here, and waited longer still for humans to discover it, then waited decades more, watching closely for every moment of every day, until at the end of this base's usage, I could determine when the most vulnerable moment would be to take the original altered sample.

"With this knowledge, I returned to the Genesis Shrine, knowing of your power and *allowing* you to once more send me back. And I waited all those trillions of years again, until I was finally at this moment once more, when the marconium will arrive from the past, completely unprotected for several more minutes.

"However now that I know what you are fully capable of, and I do not require your services again, I can simply avoid you, forever. But, I do not even need to do that. I need only evade you long enough for the marconium to arrive, at which point I will claim my prize, and reality will be mine. As I said, your presence was unplanned, but it is of no consequence." Solace's words curled as its story came to an end.

Marco continued to calculate, to plan, to think of something that might be able to stop Solace. He believed it could do what it was threatening, and therefore needed to think of a way that it couldn't. Or, maybe a reason it wouldn't.

"Hold on. If you take the marconium now, then the Shatterbug suit never gets built, which means I never receive it, and I never send you back in time to discover this base in the first place! Paradox; you would destroy yourself!" he said triumphantly.

"You think you're smarter than me; you're not." it hissed. "Time travel creates paradoxes, yes, and in a paradox situation, time attempts to repair itself as best it can, yes. But it can't quite see versions of things that have traveled across it. I lied to you at the Genesis Shrine—you could have decided to not go back in time. Your Snow Dynamics Enterprises would never have existed, your past self would be a simple college student once more, but you and I would have remained, just as we will when I create the paradox here."

As much as he hated learning his efforts in the past were recklessly built on lies, Shatterbug was confident that Solace wasn't lying here. It wouldn't, it believed it was going to survive the paradox, there's no reason to pretend it would if that were not the case. After all, it had not counted on him being here; this was its plan from the start.

"Then, once you're the 'Master of Reality,' you'll by definition be in all of space, which means it'll be even easier for me to latch my core onto you and throw you out of time!"

Again, Solace did not miss a beat. "My first act as Master of Reality will be to capture *every* single Shatterbug across *every* single moment of time in my tendrils, *drowning* them in my darkness. Shattershock all you like, I will expand to accommodate.

You may reconstitute if you must, but I am still formless, you cannot harm me. And if you try to time travel away, I will already be there, having already captured you—*all* of you. I have already won, Marco Nieve. Lie down, and perhaps I will grant you some mercy."

Marco was still conscious that he was often far too trusting of untrustworthy people, even knowing that he shouldn't believe them. Even knowing they were speaking with logic, he never enjoyed following instructions, and always worried he would regret doing so. He'd made that mistake at the Genesis Shrine, and now he was facing the consequences. He would not repeat the cycle. If Solace claimed that there was nothing he could do, now or ever, that didn't just mean he shouldn't try. If anything, it meant there was some other option that the horror was either ignorant of or protective of. He had to try anything, at every opportunity. Which meant starting right now!

"Shattershock!" Marco bellowed in the present as many times as he could, flooding the room five minutes in the past and future with Shatterbugs, all reaching and grabbing and trying to hit Solace.

It shrunk itself down to a mere thread, snaking through the air, right through their fingers, as the lone Shatterbug in the present could only watch on his visor.

"I can weave between all of you, slip through the smallest of spaces. My formlessness grants me immunity from you, Marco Nieve, and your time is running out. It will not be long now." Solace taunted.

Each of the twenty or so Shatterbugs in the future heard a faint pop, and they saw—along with the single Shatterbug still in the present, who witnessed on his visor—Solace's string-like visage jump up and out of the sea of Marcos, bolt through the air to one of the counters where a small mechanical ball, decorated with colorful wires and a small window, had appeared. However, none could get a good look, for the last thing they saw was Solace expanding just enough to crack open the machine, wrap itself around whatever was inside, and then—

Marco's vision went black. His head, his whole body, was hit by something, and the world through his eyes went dark.

Issue 12
World at Its Knees

"Marco Nieve..." a permeating voice whispered coldly into his ear.

"Wakey wakey, Marco Nieve." it said slowly, patronizingly. He grumbled in confusion, recovering from the pain in his head.

"Rouse for your Solace." the voice demanded, its words elongated cruelly, teasing him in his half-sleep.

Marco opened his eyes. He could see his visor and its blue tint, but beyond that, there was nothing. Darkness. Emptiness. Void.

He tried to move, but seemed to be surrounded completely, as if encased in concrete.

Instinctively, he held his breath, focusing desperately on not choking, trying to keep from sucking in air. He struggled against the confines of his dim prison, trying to break himself loose. He was losing oxygen.

The voice acknowledged his efforts. "Do not panic, Marco Nieve. You are restrained, but you may breathe as normal."

Running out of time, and out of energy to disobey his screaming lungs, he let in a breath of air.

Solace had not lied. It was as though he were outside. The air was thick and coarse, like he was surrounded by smoke without fire, but it was strong enough to keep him alive.

"Curious, isn't it? How something so clearly solid and opaque can allow air, and even light, to pass through it. Your lack of understanding, not only of me, but of yourself, has led you to this failure." the voice mocked him, hoarsely. "Would you like to see the glory you have ushered in?"

Solace retracted part of itself, only just enough to allow Marco to see out of his visor.

"Behold, the ruins of your city." Impossibly black tentacles latched onto and spiraled around crushed and burning buildings, snaking through the streets and over the shattered remains of long-abandoned vehicles.

"Look down at my triumphant insanity." Marco could see tendrils far and away tossing skulls and bones back and forth, toppling buildings like dominoes only to stack them back up, and grabbing at anything that might explode to bask in the fiery result.

"Gaze upon a world at its knees." On the horizon and past that, he could see only this same scene, echoed and repeated across the entire globe. An innumerable number of enormous writhing amalgamations, tearing the world apart with glee.

"My new title serves me exactly as I had hoped. Madness. Destruction. Oppression. Your world has fallen, just as I said. And it is not alone; all others are now subject to my dominion. Every planet is now blessed with my perfect psychopathy. They always have been, and they always will be. The universe is mine. Time shudders at my touch, space twists and contorts at my command, and you are powerless to stop me. Reality is powerless to stop me."

"Shatterbug!" A new voice sounded. But, this one came from within Marco's head.

Confused, he thought silently to the voice, "Are you one of my copies?"

"What? No." the voice responded inside of him. "I am controlling your will to make you believe I am in your mind."

Marco didn't respond, aloud or to himself. He was still dazed, and the strange internal voice was 'speaking' too quickly.

It sighed inside him. "I am communicating with you telepathically. There's a group of us out here, we're trying to find you. Whatever this stuff, this thing is..."

"...It's got some competition." the Hellbent finished planting in Marco Nieve's head, wherever he was.

He was trying to use his power to look for any clues as to the hero's whereabouts, but it was not something he was particularly adept at; this was not an obvious expression of his gift.

"Keep moving!" He ordered to the woman in front of him. She looked back with clear attitude on her face, but proceeded anyway, letting forth a stream of intense energy from her hands. Reactor's power was able to push the slimy black everything out of their way, allowing their little alliance of convenience to press forward.

Behind them, the man called Iceberg kept the tentacles at bay, preventing them from sweeping the group up from the rear. Furnace's powers were not very useful, as it turned out. Whatever this material was seemed to enjoy fire, even at the impressive temperatures of his abilities. He, along with Titan Black, General

Heinous, and the Hellbent, walked in the middle of their small bubble of safety. A moving eye in an endless storm.

Life had always been like this, the Hellbent knew that. And yet it all seemed so unfamiliar, so new and surprising. He knew who Shatterbug was, and knew that he hated him, but he had never known him, never met Marco Nieve. It was as though he had two sets of memories, neither strong enough to overcome the other.

Still, his contradicting thoughts agreed: this superhero was their best chance at stopping this nightmare. If it was a nightmare. He knew of Shatterbug's powers. He could go back in time, prevent this from happening. If it had a beginning to prevent.

Eventually, Reactor reached a point that refused to bend to her light. It squealed in denial, holding its ground against her. It took the shape of a ball at the edge of their rebellion, holding something within it.

"Push harder!" the Hellbent ordered.

"I'm trying!" she shouted back, her powers growing with annoyance and fury. All around the large sphere, the shadowy tentacles retreated into the larger masses, but the orb remained.

"We have to crack that mass! He must be in there!"

The behemoth called Titan Black pushed past the Hellbent, aware of his huge size and therefore treading gently around the much smaller people.

"Stop." he said quietly, which for him was a low rumble.

Reactor halted her attack. The tentacles returned to the sides of the sphere, but were hesitant to advance any closer.

"Stand aside." Black ordered the woman. She did what was asked of her, allowing the walking corpse to face the floating hole of darkness alone.

He wound his fist back, and then with a thundering roar, he threw his whole massive weight into one punch, slamming into the ball of tentacles with extreme prejudice.

They hissed and screeched with a horrifying and painful echo of whispers and screams, but unfurled themselves, having been met with a match for their resilience: their own blood.

From the unlatching walls of voidlike tendrils, the shape of a man fell to the ground, safe in the small space of allies. He wore a blue suit that was covered in plates, and his helmet was reminiscent of an astronaut's, though much more sleek and round. He coughed briefly, getting his bearings as he stood up to face his rescuers.

"Visor off."

Marco was free of Solace's prison, but was confused as to the new situation he found himself in.

Before him, all of the villains he had faced in these past few months looked upon him, surrounded on all sides by the perfect blackness of this horrible new reality.

"Hellbent?" Marco said, at a loss for words. "And Heinous, Titan Black...? What are you all doing here?"

"We've been searching for you, to ask for your help." the Hellbent replied.

"I have failed to save humanity. As I predicted, a great barrier has come that we were not prepared for." the General added.

"We can't destroy the world while this thing exists." Reactor spoke for her Disaster Pact.

"None of us want the same thing." Titan Black said in a quiet rumble. "But we're all in agreement; we don't want this. We need you to save us, Shatterbug. Go back in time; stop this *ajeno* from doing to the world what it did to me."

"I..." Marco said, a swell of pride caught in his throat. It fell quickly, sinking into his stomach. "I can't. There's nothing I can do. This thing, Solace— it got access to time travel. It's not just everywhere, it's everywhen. My powers are useless against it now."

"It seems to believe otherwise. It had you trapped; we haven't found anyone else in that state." Furnace spoke up.

"Right, and now this—you called it Solace? It isn't trying to swallow us up." Reactor noted. "We've been moving through it with mine and Iceberg's powers, but now it's keeping its distance."

"There's one thing I can do to stop it: if I can touch any part of it with my marconium core, I can cast it through time. But it knows that. It had me trapped so I couldn't move, but now that I'm free, it'll keep its distance." he said solemnly.

"So we must work together." The Hellbent was standing tall, unfazed, like a true leader. "You seem to know more about this Solace than us. How is it doing this? We may be able to figure out a plan to end this."

"I suppose we can try." the hero began, unconvinced but optimistic. "Solace exists in every moment of time, thanks to a version of my marconium core taken from the past. It can time travel faster and more efficiently than my suit; it's practically omnitemporal.

"It's also using this thing called a Universal Model to open portals across all of space for it to reach through, basically making it omnipresent."

"Portals, you say?" General Heinous asked, an air of curiosity evident in her artificial speech generator.

"Yeah, I guess maybe it can't get big enough on its own? Or maybe it's just using the Model to be more aware of itself across the whole universe."

"Yes, I had gathered that." the General said shortly. "But if it is using portals, is it possible that we could follow through one? Reach it somehow?"

"That could work." the Hellbent said in endorsement of the cyborg's plan. "It must have a central system, all lifeforms do. If it is on the other end of one of these wormholes, we can fight it at its most vulnerable."

"And also its most powerful!" Iceberg spoke up now, unsure of this bold objective. "We're only barely keeping these parts of it at bay. And we know it can hold its own if it tries. What chance do we stand when we have its full attention?"

"None. Titan Black, on the other hand..." suggested the Hellbent.

"Of course! You said Solace did something to you! You have some of its power!" Shatterbug realized in excitement.

"Not gonna work either." the hulking brute muttered, hanging his head. "Like you said, this *monstruo* will be more powerful at the source. It literally pumped my veins full of itself, it is my blood. If it thinks I'm a threat, no way it's gonna let me keep that. I'm easier to kill than any of you; and you're all real easy to kill, *hombres.*"

"We have to try something, and at the moment, this appears to be the best option." the General said, pulling the group together. "We either die fighting for humanity, or starve allowing this to continue. I for one do not want to see this world suffer a second longer. I will confront Solace."

She looked around at the alliance of convenience, as if waiting for someone else to add something. Finally, Shatterbug broke the silence.

"I will confront Solace." he said, with honesty and conviction unrivaled.

The Hellbent turned his masked head to look at the hero he somehow despised and admired all at once. He nodded his head, submitting to the will of the man he strangely thought of as an old friend. "I will confront Solace."

Reactor smacked the backs of both Furnace and Iceberg, nudging them into the fold. Together the three agreed with dignity. "I will confront Solace."

The alliance turned to the looming shape of their foe's former slave, killed and forced to go on in pain. He tried to avert their gaze, but slowly allowed a smirk to creep on the side of his face. He looked into Marco's eyes, unabated by his retracted visor. "I will confront Solace."

"Then it's settled." the General observed. "We must find one of these portals."

"Shouldn't be too hard, there must be hundreds in New Jackson alone."

"But they'll all be protected, if we can even fit through them."

"Solace could be filling up as much of the holes as it can. Greedy *pendejo*."

"We can push past it, we can do this!"

The villains, led by their hero, continued moving through the transformed streets of New Jackson. They had lived with this torment all their lives; or at least, they believed they had, from Marco's perspective. He wasn't sure what they were all doing here, how the city was even standing at all in this new timeline, but his focus for now was on finding a portal to the Genesis Shrine.

It was difficult to see anything, though. New Jackson was a very flat state, and the capital city was no exception. Where San Francisco had hills, the roads and buildings here were constructed on a flat plane, courtesy of the deserts of the western United States. Unable to get to higher ground outside, even Titan Black was only barely able to see over the enormous walls of Solace's omnipresence.

Near the tops of the many skyscrapers, Marco thought he could just see the ends of some tentacles protruding from nowhere, or passing through points in the air, only to vanish. If these were portals, they were much too high to reach, and they opened and closed quickly and without pattern.

The entourage moved northward, though they were unaware of their direction, as the sun was only a glimmer through the smoky sky, and the horizon was concealed by the tallest of Solace's masses. Finally, they happened upon the intersection at

Central Avenue and Fillmore Street. None of the others recognized the significance, but Shatterbug immediately knew where he was.

"Snow Dynamics." he said in humble admiration.

"What was that?" the Hellbent asked.

"Sorry, nothing." Marco looked up, craning to see the top of the twenty-four story building. "Just a memory."

Titan Black, too, was looking at the top of the tower. He did not need to crane his neck as much, but did so anyway. "I see something up there."

"What is it?" General Heinous asked in synthetic interest.

They all tried to look now, backing up to get a better angle. Furnace even tried to jump to get a better view.

Inspired by this, the General activated her rocket implants, rising up just a few feet to get any sense of what Black had seen. From her new vantage point, she was able to make out that a number of fat tendrils, which stretched high over their heads and around the other nearby buildings, were crawling and expanding out from the top of this one. They were snaking and writhing out of nowhere; there was no source.

But of course, she knew there was.

"There's a portal up there. A permanent one, from the looks of it." She informed her party.

"Of course there is." Marco said, not amused by the irony. Solace was far too much of a performer, it was nauseating.

"We need to get up there. Heinous, can you lift us?" The Hellbent looked to the General as she descended back to Earth.

"Sadly not; the thrusters aren't capable of expelling as much fuel all at once as it would take to lift two people." She turned to the Titan. "And *he* would definitely be out of the question."

"So we gotta climb, then." Iceberg declared.

"It seems there's no alternative. I don't see any other permanent portals nearby. We need to take our chances with this one." answered the Hellbent.

"I wonder if Solace knows what we're planning." Reactor thought aloud.

"No way it doesn't. It would be keeping a close eye on him." Black remarked, nodding towards Marco. "Probably looking through my eye, in fact."

"What? You're saying you're a spy?" questioned an alarmed Furnace.

"You think he isn't?" Shatterbug said with annoyance. "He's got some of Solace inside of him, you knew this already. If it can, it is; we have to assume that. That doesn't change that he's trying to help us."

Furnace grumbled something incoherently, but proceeded into the skyscraper anyway, leading the charge. The other villains, one by one, followed in line. Shatterbug and Iceberg entered last, the latter holding up the rear.

Unsurprisingly, Snow Dynamics Enterprises was no less occupied. It was empty, though. There had never been a Snow Dynamics. Only Solace's tentacles lined the walls, caked the floors, and hung from the ceilings. Reactor kept them at bay, but the tendrils were much more aggressive now, getting the hint as to where the allies were heading.

"It's twenty-four stories up, then to the roof." Marco informed his team. This was like the Ivory Tower from Terminus 2. He hoped it wouldn't be as time consuming as that questline. Presumably, Solace wouldn't be any more powerful as they got higher, and it wasn't like they would have to actually pass through each floor; they could stay in the stairwell the whole way up. "The stairs are forward and to the left, past the elevators."

Reactor nodded and moved forward, letting her hands move around much more here than when they were outside, keeping the dancing tentacles, taunting them like cobras, at bay.

When any of these appendages inevitably got in, Titan Black was able to crush them enough that they would retreat back out of their circle of safety.

Iceberg was much better at maintaining the rear than Reactor was at holding up the front. Of course, his powers could be spread out more, whereas Reactors were bound to beams of light.

They opened the door to the staircase, finding it pitch black. Reactor was able to illuminate the walls as she aimed her energy streams up and around, but the darkness' presence was strong, here. And as there were no windows in the stairwell, and no working lights, her power provided their only hope of visibility.

Solace had tendrils lining the floors and stairs like a maze of undergrowth. They would slink away in pain at Reactor's light, but she couldn't focus on the ground and on the walls ahead of them.

To rectify this, Titan Black led the way now—after breaking down the door to allow his massive form through—with Reactor close behind, firing off her energy around and in front of the behemoth. As he stepped on the shadowy flooring, it retreated under the massive weight of its own kind, returning to the walls as they were pushed back and away from the line of climbing humans.

They followed Black and Reactor up, stopping every few floors to catch their breath. They were moving slowly, but doing so while going up so many stairs only made the energy requirement more demanding.

After some time, they reached the door to the roof. Shatterbug turned to his strange companions.

"Once we open this door, there's no telling what will happen. It could realize what we're doing and immediately kill us, before Reactor has a chance to hold it back. It might seem like it lets us through the portal, only to pick us off as we enter. We need to be on our guard, be ready for anything."

The assembled villains nodded in understanding, readying themselves.

Titan Black smashed through the door.

Reactor aimed her hands out onto the roof, prepared to fire.

The tentacles on the roof, from this angle, were now clearly coming from the other side of a floating hole in the world. It was like a rippling pool of purple, silver, and gold liquids, sitting vertically in the air. It was much larger than the one Marco had passed through before, and lacked the black frame of swirling tendrils that Solace had used to hold it open. This one kept its shape thanks to the fat tentacles squirming out of it and across the city. Each must have been six or seven feet in diameter, and they stretched out across the skyline to the nearby buildings. It was difficult to tell, as they were so impossibly black that they lacked any texture, but it looked like more and more of their length was crawling out from the portal. They seemed uninterested in the alliance's presence.

Reactor led the way for them to move closer, with Shatterbug close behind. She wasn't using her power, but kept her palms trained on the black masses all around them, ready to defend the group.

As they reached the portal, Marco held out a hand to touch it.

Suddenly, it vanished.

The entire portal collapsed in on itself in an instant, just before Marco could pass through. The tentacles it granted passage to seemed to be gone, but not even a moment later, they reappeared, sprawling across the skyline, emerging from a new portal. The rippling hole now stood on the roof of the next closest skyscraper, about half a block away.

"No!" Marco shouted in frustration, trying to hold back tears of anger. "No, no, no!"

He collapsed, falling to his knees, his fists balled.

"There's nothing we can do." he said to the teammates behind him, devastated. "There's nothing I can do. This is the end."

"This is far from the end, Marco." said a simple voice, sounding from in front of the hero.

Marco looked up. As he did, he first saw a pair of polished black shoes. His eyes rose higher, seeing just the bottom of grey pant legs, before they became concealed by a long, grey, woolen cloak. Two arms held their hands in the coat's pockets, and as the wool ended at the collar, a darker grey suit was just visible beneath the head of the outfit's wearer. It was a plain and unremarkable head, and yet it was so simple, so unimpressive, that it was inexplicably stunning and commanding of attention.

"Null?"

The man in grey nodded, as a friend.

"What are you doing here? You should be in your universe, keeping it safe!" Marco said with concern.

"My universe is not under siege. This being—"

"Solace." Marco clarified for the unusually typical man.

"Ah, yes. Solace. It appears to be unique to this one. And I have therefore come to help. Which leads me back to this: this is not the end, Marco. You have faced this horror before, yes? Surely you must know a way to stop it?"

"We've already been over this, *chico.*" Titan Black growled with annoyance.

"It's alright, Black." Marco said, turning back to him. "I defeated it once, or I thought I had. Just delayed the inevitable I guess. It's a monster that can shapeshift to any size, any shape, even change its mass. It's insane, and it just wants to enslave; I don't think it even has a reason. It has time travel now, and it's using something called the Universal Model to be everywhere at once. With both of those, it effectively controls time and space. Even without that, it has contingencies upon contingencies, it is so careful and so well-prepared, I don't think even Timegaze can stop it."

Null thought for a moment before replying. "But you say it shapeshifts, and this Universal Model, it is a device, a transporter? So with those two facts combined, it is seemingly everywhere at once. And that is true for every moment of time. That seems to imply, it must have a core, some sort of base, stationed at the Model."

"We came to that conclusion as well." the Hellbent said coldly.

"Guys, relax." Shatterbug scolded the team. "He wasn't here for that, let him work it out."

"Thank you, Marco." Null smiled warmly. "Now, if that is so, I have an idea. If we can fight it, hurt it, if only enough that we can make it flinch where it is most vulnerable, we can push it through a portal into my universe, trapping it there. I can set into effect my contingencies, destroying that world, and Solace with it."

Marco jerked with the implications of this plan. "Unacceptable. I'm not letting you destroy your world."

"This is about more than my world, Marco, or even yours." the man in grey tried to calm his heroic acquaintance. "If Solace is half as powerful and intelligent as you claim, it will eventually realize there exists other worlds beyond these two, other universes. And if it truly is so insane and so driven by oppression, it will seek out a way to do to them what has been done here, and it will find one. I would much rather sacrifice an artificial world to save all natural ones."

The hero of time thought long and hard. Null was talking about more than murder, more than genocide. It would be the extinction of an entire universe. People he knew lived there— albeit only duplicates of them—and billions, maybe trillions of lifeforms that he didn't know. Who was he to decide their fate, to determine whether they were worthy of existence? Could he choose to damn them just to save his own world from one creature, even one as powerful and cruel as Solace?

It was a decision he did not want to be responsible for. One he felt there was no right answer to. If he allowed it, a world of worlds teeming with life would be extinguished in an instant. But, if he didn't, he may as well be dooming what remained of his home to an eternity of suffering and psychosis. That seemed just as bad in his mind.

And yet, Null made a good point. Marco hadn't even known there existed other universes before now. If Solace didn't already, it was bound to find out eventually. He would be actively condemning all of them to this torment if he refused.

Finally, still unsure, but recognizing the necessity of the plan, Marco agreed. "If you say so…"

He looked back to the convenient alliance, each of them bowing their heads in respect, silently conferring to the hero their reluctant support in his choice.

"Where is this Universal Model, then? I can create a portal to take us there and confront this horror."

"A place called the Genesis Shrine." Marco answered, still shaken. "Solace said it was where the universe is born and burned, over and over again."

"Ah, yes, it's right in the name. Genesis. It is the center of the universe, where it was born in the big bang. Let's go, all of you."

Marco blinked.

When his eyes opened, along with the eyes of his teammates, he stood once more in the Genesis Shrine, at the center of the universe. Where the big bang had created all matter, and where it would supposedly all fall into, only to be exploded back out into the darkness.

Solace was here, as everywhere. While its many tendrils, ranging from mere threads to fat, crushing appendages snaked and slunk all over the pillars and floors of the monument, its main form was hovering beside the Model at the center of the room. An innumerable number of tentacles poked at and arced in an out of the ball of dancing lights—the map of all creation. The smallest portals here translating to enormous rifts through which the horrible psychopath exerted its tyranny onto the universe.

Its central mass seemed to turn, as much as a shapeless, textureless void could appear to, and face its visitors.

"Ah, you have returned, Marco Nieve." it hummed with its calculated, bemused growl. Marco had gotten used to it, and annoyed with it by now. As for the others—Marco could feel the chill in the air, as Solace's haunting presence shook their very beings. Even Titan Black, who had met this monster before, shuddered his engorged muscles in fear of his inhuman master. "Have you and your friends come to worship your new God?"

"You are no God, Solace." Marco was able to assert. He no longer wanted to play Solace's games. They had a plan, and they would succeed.

"Indeed." it replied with a low grumble, exaggerating the word even more than usual. "God implies omnibenevolence, and though I am many things, benevolent is not one of them. So then, you have come to die. How... disappointing. I had hoped you would be more grateful for the gift of continued life."

"What do you mean by that, abomination?" General Heinous shouted up at the eldritch overlord, the volume of her voice synthesizer turned up to the highest setting.

It growled hoarsely before responding. "Are you still so ignorant? All of you? I am the Master of Reality! In every moment, paradoxes threaten to rip the fabrics of time and space apart. The whole universe screams in agony, threatening to collapse in on itself; but, I have taken on the responsibility of the De'Raj, maintaining reality, keeping it safe. In my image. Do you see, now? *Nothing* and *no one* exists now, without my express approval. You should all have been erased, yet you endure because I *will* it, so great is my power."

"You've explained nothing." the Hellbent interjected, angrily. "We are here because of you, but why? Cruel entertainment?"

"Call it... parental compassion."

"I'm sorry?" Titan Black blurted, holding back a laugh, yet still betrayed by the sounds of fear.

"I am responsible for many of you becoming what you are, now. Titan Black was spawned from my glory directly, but even the Hellbent is a product of my subtle influences. I have some... emotional attachment to you. Also, and for those of you I did not rear, you are simply of no threat to me."

Null appeared to fly up now, out of the crowd of rebels, right in front of the 'face' of Solace—though Marco assumed there was some other in-depth explanation for this motion. He spoke shortly and coldly to the chaotic horror. "And what of me, Solace?"

"You..." it said, again elongating the word even by its own standards. It growled, as if with a concerned familiarity.

"So you know who I am, then?"

"Yes... I know you..." Solace said slowly, reacting slightly upon recognizing the man in grey—but not even Null was certain as to why.

"Then you know what I can do." he said confidently.

Its words curled now as normal, as if its mouth, if it had one, was smiling knowingly. "I know you can only create, not destroy. You are helpless here."

"I may not be able to destroy, but I can create things that can. I can create a hundred mechanisms and forces to kill you here, at this moment."

"And if you do, one of my selves existing in the past will prevent it, creating a paradox that I will once again mend as I see fit." it responded with surety.

Solace let out a shrieking howl, a deep sigh that seemed to reverberate inwards and across the whole of its formlessness—across the whole of creation. It echoed through the fabrics of the universe, ruthlessly mocking the assembled mortals.

"Shattershock!" Marco let out; his signal to begin the attack against the tyrant of reality.

As his duplicates in the past and future came into being, all three Shatterbugs saw their alliance of convenience releasing their combined wrath upon the body of Solace all across the Shrine.

He shattershocked three more times from his present self, and in the past and future, four Marcos leapt onto tentacles all around them, not trying to do anything in particular other than distract. To hold Solace's attention.

General Heinous flew into the air, her thrusters sending her flying around the room as she let out rounds of bullets across the battlefield and into the shapeless void of Solace. It was impossible to tell if her shots were landing, or if the impossible darkness was even damaged, but it was clearly affected somehow. Dozens of tendrils reached into the air like spikes, lashing, swiping, and thrusting all around to try to bring the cyborg down.

One of these wide tentacles threatened to come crashing down on the General's head, but one of the Marcos in the future foresaw this, and shouted to her. "Heinous, barrel roll!"

She looked at him quickly, before following the hero's suggestion, tucking to the left. In her spin, she saw the blackness fall down where she had just been, before completing her rotation and regaining her orientation safely. She gave a thumbs up to Marco—although not the one which had warned her—before continuing her assault.

As Solace's tentacles moved its whole form about, flailing up and all around at the air, Null created new walls, ever closer to the primary mass, aiming to box it into one corner.

The Hellbent's powers were not particularly useful in this battle. Solace's will was too powerful, too inhuman, and too everywhere to be controlled. Still, his suit allowed him to take much more of a beating from the slimy, heaving tendrils. They still knocked him around and flung him about, but he was hardly hurt by it. Not hurt enough to need to rest, anyway. He wrestled with a larger mass, before being pulled away to box with a wall of prodding shadows. He was by no means winning, but he didn't have to.

Of course, Solace didn't know that. It considered all of them a threat now, and so it slowly began to wrap itself around the Hellbent's legs, chaining him to the ground. It latched onto his arms, holding back his punches and grabs. As one last thread began to wrap itself around his neck to choke him, he saw something from the corner of his eye.

"Brace for impact! Reconstitute!" Shatterbug shouted at him. He closed his eyes and tensed his muscles, and as the hero's fist collided with the chin of his mask, the force of nine Shatterbugs uniting in time sent him flying out of Solace's grips, into the air.

The Hellbent landed on the steps leading up to the Universal Model, dazed, but free.

"Thank you, Marco." he willed Shatterbug's mind into believing he had said to him. The hero nodded his helmet, before shattershocking four more times, rejoining the fight.

On either side of the Hellbent, two new barriers were created, sprouting up from the ground, cutting off three quarters of the arena. He leapt from his perch to continue his assault on the shrinking form of their oppressor.

The Disaster Pact was struggling against Solace at its core. On Earth, they were facing mere fingers, the vestiges of a greater power. This was the hand, the body of the horror and oppression they had lived in their entire lives. Or thought they had. Reactor and Iceberg could keep the masses back, but Furnace's powers were worse than useless; they almost seemed to feed the beast. He tried to keep his powers trained on the tentacles, but they only seemed to follow the fire, until they came so close that one of his comrades would need to open themselves up briefly just to save him.

They were doing their best to confine as much of Solace's shape into one portion of the room, but this constant interruption of their harmony was setting them back more and more each time.

Finally, the primary mass of their foe was in such a position that the trio was equidistant from each other on three sides of the monster, with the fourth back side up against the open window out into space. However, the tendrils still followed Furnace's fire, bolstered by it, enabling Solace to hold firm against Reactor and Iceberg.

Furnace heard shouting behind him. "Cross the streams, Vince! Use your power with theirs!"

He turned to see Shatterbug, jumping up and down, trying to get his attention.

"Cross the streams?" he muttered to himself in confusion. He shrugged, figuring the choice was moot.

He aimed his hands—and the streams of fire expanding from them—at the points at which his partners' abilities were impacting with the creature.

At Reactor's side, the light energy ignited, as though it was composed of supercharged combustible, unlit particles. Its power seemed to increase staggeringly, as Solace shrieked in pain at the new sensation.

On Iceberg's end, the freezing air boiled, becoming a scalding flow of raw elements, causing the psychopathic void to retreat further into itself.

Solace now hovered as a single mass of writhing tendrils, growling loudly as the Disaster Pact continued to restrain its malleable formlessness.

Furnace thought he saw a blink of light come from the space between the pillars that Solace was held against.

Marco turned to the man now called Titan Black.

"You ready, Julio?"

"I got this, *hermano.*" He stood in front of Marco, between him and the main collective of Solace.

Marco pulled back his fist, then as it swung in towards the dead, contracting flesh of the behemoth, he exclaimed with finality. "Reconstitute!"

Nine Marcos came together, back into a single moment of time, combining their forces into one fluid motion. The impact sent Black flying, straight into Solace's still-screaming body.

Black extended his own fist as he quickly approached the horror, pushing his legs into the ground, creating wakes in the floor in an attempt to slow his advance. Null assisted in this as well, cushioning the ground in front of him to help get the brute to just the right speed.

He could feel Solace trying to revoke its curse upon him, to return him to his death, but it was unable to focus enough, to finish fast enough.

His fist collided with the slimy material of the cruel master's void, sending it catapulting out and into the space between the pillars of the Shrine.

Then, as if a gate suddenly closed, it vanished. The same scene was visible through the open window, but Solace was gone.

Solace pulled itself back into the Genesis Shrine, no longer being bombarded by the mortals' annoying abilities. It had underestimated their teamwork, but they had no hope of stopping it. It was having some difficulty ending the fight, yes, but it was only humoring them anyway. Playing with its food.

As it hovered back into the room, it noticed that the little humans were no longer present. Not even Marco Nieve.

"Ah, so they were smart enough to retreat, to regroup. How quaint." it said, admiring the solidity of its conclusion. They were gone, and it still had the marconium. It was still in control.

It returned its attention, and many tendrils, to the Universal Model, eager to continue maintaining the paradoxes and oppressing what remained of the universe.

As it approached the ball of lights though, it stopped itself short. It hovered there, confused, staring into the Model as the realization slowly hit it.

The lights within the sphere were coming closer together. The ball was shrinking. The universe was collapsing.

"No, no this is not acceptable!" it howled, stretching its tentacles and arcing them into the Model.

All across the universe, it gripped its enormous tendrils, larger than it had ever wielded, around entire planets. It pushed back against suns, wrapped itself around every individual asteroid. Solace did everything it could to keep everything where it was, to hold reality together.

However, the forces were too strong. Reality was converging on it, falling into the center of the universe. Falling directly into Solace.

"Stay... where... you... are...!" it shouted at absolutely everything, in every time. No matter how far back it went, how much of itself filled every unoccupied space, the Model did not stop shrinking.

"I will not die! I cannot die!" Solace screamed. It let out a noise that could only be described as its equivalent of weeping, of sobbing.

In only a few moments, every single planet in the universe, every single sun and asteroid and black hole was forced into a single point of reality. In just one second, the whole universe, with Solace trapped inside, was dead.

"So that's that, then?" Reactor was the first to speak.

"Indeed." Null said, furrowing his brow. "I cannot open a window back into my world. It's gone."

"And Solace with it." the Hellbent said, his tone reminding them of their triumph. The reason for their sacrifice.

"What now?" Titan Black asked no one in particular.

"We return to our lives." General Heinous answered. She turned to Marco. "Make no mistake, this alliance was only out of the necessity of the situation. I will still save humanity from itself, with or without you."

"I'm counting on it." he replied with ironic sincerity.

"I will take us back to Ear—"

"Wait!" Shatterbug shouted.

"Jeez, relax." Iceberg said, rubbing his ears.

"What's wrong, Marco?" Null said with concern.

"This place, the Genesis Shrine. Its protectors are dead. We can't just leave it."

218

"Are you volunteering?" Furnace said, elbowing Iceberg in amusement.

Marco huffed and shook his head. "No, no. I'm saying we need to destroy it."

They all turned their heads, looking at each other, unsure of who was supposed to respond.

With everyone else milling in silence, Null took it upon himself to concur first. "I agree. This Model, without its guardians, is too dangerous to be left alone. Its only purpose now would be for evil, and so it cannot be allowed to remain. I will open a portal from Earth for the Disaster Pact to fire into. They will obliterate it, and I will seal the portal before the fallout reaches the hole."

"Fair enough." Reactor said, nodding in agreement.

Null did as he said. A portal opened through which each member of the temporary team walked through, one by one. They turned to face it, to face into the Genesis Shrine for the final time.

Furnace, Iceberg, and Reactor united their attacks, each letting forth a bursting stream of destruction, converging on the Universal Model. The explosion ripped the monument apart, toppling pillars and cracking the roof, but no one was able to get a good look at the ruins. Null closed the gateway before the fires reached them, cutting them off from the desolation.

Marco turned to thank everyone, but the Hellbent, General Heinous, and Titan Black had already gone. Only Null and the Disaster Pact remained.

"Well, we'll be seeing you." Iceberg said, gripping Marco's gloved hand firmly.

"Uh, yeah, I hope not." he said, unsurely.

"Oh I dunno. We've got a kind of newfound respect for existence." Reactor said, smiling. "Our powers destroy, but that doesn't mean we have to."

She hugged Marco, and Furnace gave him a casual salute, before the three walked off in each other's arms. They behaved like siblings. Trauma did have a way of bringing people together.

"And what about you, Null? Are you going to create another copy world?" he asked, turning to the man in grey.

"No, I don't think that is necessary anymore." he responded distantly, looking away from Marco. "And anyway, I don't think the answers I seek will be found anywhere but here. Solace was unique to this world, like you. But, if it is the reason you are unique, then why is it unique? Perhaps it had something to do with me, and with them."

"I don't think it matters, *amigo*." Marco said gently, trying to relax Null's mind.

"Perhaps not to you. But my power, my whole identity, relies on understanding. I will keep searching." He turned to the hero, smiling slightly. "For now, though, I will celebrate this victory. This universe, and all others, were saved this day. I thank you for that, Marco Nieve."

The peculiarly plain man held out his white-gloved hand.

Marco reached out to shake it firmly, but vigorously. "Thank you, Null."

Marco blinked.

aaaaaaaabbbbbbbbbbbbbbbbbbbbcccccddeeeeeee
aaaaaaaaabbbbbbbbbbb
aaaaabbbbbbbbbbbbbbbbbbbbbcccccccccccccc
aaaaaaaaaaaaaa
aaaaaaaa aaaaaabbbbbbbbbbbbbbbbbbbccccccccccccccccccc
aaaaaaaaaaaaaaabbbbbbbbbbbbbbbbbbbbbcccccccccccc
aaaaaaaaaaaaaaaaaaabbbbb

www.ingramcontent.com/pod-product-compliance
Lightning Source LLC
Chambersburg PA
CBHW050922120626
46552CB00018B/1787